ABOUT THIS BOOK

From *USA Today* Bestselling Author Morgan Wylie - She's a lead witch assassin—until he leads her to question everything she's ever believed.

Hollis Blackstone is a lead assassin for her father's rogue band of witch hunters. For longer than she can remember, her father, Dante, has had two missions: rid the world of witches and locate his estranged family kept from him by his sister's rebellion. Working off a lead, Hollis finds her way through the mysterious borders of Havenwood Falls. Her father's orders were to gather intel on the whereabouts of all the Blackstones, all the witches, and the seat of their power. But then she meets the irresistible Ryne Calloway.

Half witch and half phoenix, Ryne hasn't been in Havenwood Falls for long. Rejected by his father's clan because of his witch heritage, he knows all about suppressing who he really is. In town for a fresh start, he hopes to relax and have fun. And that's exactly what he plans to do with the pretty new girl who strolled into town with a stick up her butt.

Ryne opens Hollis's eyes, widening her perspective beyond the hatred she's been taught. But when her father seeks her out, everything begins to unravel. She's finally found someone who loves her for her, but she's about to lose him before ever having the chance to love him back.

HAVENWOOD FALLS BOOKS

Forget You Not by Kristie Cook

Old Wounds by Susan Burdorf

Fate, Love & Loyalty by E.J. Fechenda

The Winged & the Wicked by T.V. Hahn & Kristie Cook

Alpha's Queen by Lila Felix

Ink & Fire by R.K. Ryals

Lose You Not by Kristie Cook

Tragic Ink by Heather Hildenbrand

Nowhere to Hide by Belinda Boring

Flames Among the Frost by Amy Hale

Rock Me Gently by Susan Burdorf

From the Embers by Amy Miles

Defying Gravity by Kallie Ross

Break Me Not by Kristie Cook

How the Dead Lie by Stacey Rourke

The Lurkers Within by Danielle Bannister

The Collector: Awakening by Kristie Cook, R.K. Ryals, Belinda Boring & Nadirah Foxx

Addicted to You by Belinda Boring

Affliction Mine by C.J. Pinard

The Ward & the Wanderers by T.V. Hahn

Toil & Trouble by Melissa Wright

Of Salt and Stars by Seven Jane

Redefined by Morgan Wylie

Betrayal Among the Frost by Amy Hale

Forever Loyal by E.J. Fechenda

Fate's Demand by Emily Cyr

The Wu & the Wand by T.V. Hahn

A Demon's Redemption by JD Nelson

Also try the YA line, Havenwood Falls High; the historical paranormal line, Legends of Havenwood Falls; the darker, sexier side of town, Havenwood Falls Sin & Silk; and the local supernatural college, Sun & Moon Academy.

Stay up to date at www.HavenwoodFalls.com

BOOKS BY MORGAN WYLIE

YA FANTASY

Silent Orchids (Book 1)

Veiled Shadows (Book 2)

Daegan (Novella 2.5)

Fractured Darkness (Book 3)

Fading Light (Book 4)

The Sol-lumieth (Book 5) (Winter 2019)

The Rise of the Paladin (An Alandria Short Story Prequel) (Free with Newsletter subscription)

YA PARANORMAL/SUPERNATURAL

HAILEY: The Necromancer (A Shadow Realm Novella 1)

(previously released as Supernatural Chronicles: The Necromancers Novella #7)

JAX: The Doppelgänger (A Shadow Realm Novella 2)

WILLOW (A Shadow Realm Novella 3) (Coming soon!)

SOLANGE (A Shadow Realm Novella 4) (Coming soon!)

NA/ADULT PARANORMAL ROMANCE

RYLEN (The Tangled Web Book 1)

MATHER (The Tangled Web Book 2)

JET (A Tangled Web Novella)

HAVENWOOD FALLS

Reawakened (A Havenwood Falls High Novella)

Dawn of the Witch Hunters (A Legends of Havenwood Falls Novella)

Redefined (A Havenwood Falls Novella)

Rise of the Witch Hunters (A Legends of Havenwood Falls Novella)
(Coming Fall 2019)

REDEFINED

A HAVENWOOD FALLS NOVELLA

MORGAN WYLIE

To anyone who needs a second chance. To anyone who needs to redefine who they are. You got this!

CHAPTER 1

*H*ollis Blackstone stared at herself in her bedroom mirror, seeing only the assassin she had been created to be, wondering if there was anything else she might ever become. She had quickly gained the position as one of the lead assassins for her father, Dante Blackstone. Being a witch hunter was more than her job; it was her entire life, day and night. Hollis had been training to be the best since she could remember. On nights when the teams ransacked home after home, she caught a rare glimpse of him smiling at her—at what she'd accomplished—and she believed him to be proud of her. The teams liked to make a mess of each witch's home they attacked, but Hollis preferred her team to be stealthy, more deadly. The lack of interruption to one's home seemed to send a greater message than a tantrum of violent proportions.

Her room was nothing more than an empty shell, a cavern of unrealized possibilities. Hollis didn't waste time decorating her rooms, for there would always be another, in another town. Her father's organization—her family—moved around more often than they stayed in one place, or so it seemed the past year or so. Plus it was just one more thing to have to worry about, to take her focus away from her job—her obsession.

Pulling on her black leather jacket, despite the early May warm weather, she covered the multiple tattoos on her shoulders stretching down toward her elbows. Hollis fluffed her long dark hair in the mirror, checking to ensure the scar at her hairline was hidden, and made sure she was presentable. She had been called in to see her father, and he didn't tolerate sloppiness or tardiness. Dante always dressed impeccably to impress and to intimidate, and he expected nothing less from his teams. An inept capability to be present when requested was unacceptable to Dante.

They had only recently set up this home, and Hollis didn't even remember what city they were in this time, but she knew they were somewhere near Santa Fe, New Mexico. Dear old dad had been chasing a lead in his lifelong obsession to track down the other Blackstones—those he considered lost and in need of his guidance— and the secret place in which they lived. About a year and a half ago, they had almost found it, but somehow it mysteriously—most likely magically—slipped through their fingers, and they couldn't remember anything about where they had been or where they were trying to get. Her father had been infuriated.

He had been on a rampage ever since they had let Macy Blackstone—who'd been staying with them—get away. Macy had been the biggest lead they'd had in a long time. Her father received slight pulls in the right direction, which he could never describe other than to say he "sensed the spirit of his sister Marie and the rest of his family who *should* be with him." At other times, Dante would utter vague accounts of being so close to the name of the town in his mind only to have it slip away like a lost memory he tried to force to the surface. Somehow they still mysteriously received secret letters from Aunt Letti to Grace and the other old gals no matter where they were, but her teams could never trace the letters' origins.

Hollis strode down the hall with purpose and ownership, stopping only when she arrived at her dad's office. Knocking twice, she didn't wait long. He was straight to business as he called through the door.

"Come in, daughter mine," Dante called through the door, his voice strong and sure. It could have been one of several of the

Blackstones who lived with them at the door, but he seemed to always know when Hollis was near. Dante had lived a long time and been quite prolific with reproduction over the span. Even Grace, who appeared to be in her seventies and was half hunter and half human, was one of his descendants. Hollis refused to consider them all siblings since the ages varied so drastically, but they were family just the same. Right as Hollis turned the handle, a young girl in her early teen years with golden blond hair skipped around the corner.

"Have fun, Hollis!" Sunny called with a singsong voice and a big smile.

Hollis didn't let anyone close, but if anyone could get under her skin and attach themselves to her, it was Sunny. Sunny had a way about her that would disarm the most hardened criminal. The family referred to her as their "little ray of caffeinated sunshine." Hollis reached out and tugged on one of Sunny's pigtails.

"Thanks, kid. See ya 'round."

"Maybe, maybe not," she continued in her singsong tone and shrugged. Sunny suddenly stopped and then frowned. Her expression sobered, then she stared into Hollis's eyes. "I'll miss you, but I'm happy for you." Sunny came in for a quick, unexpected hug, then turned without another word. She skipped down the hallway, leaving Hollis with a dumbfounded look on her face.

"What was that about?" Hollis wondered under her breath.

"Are you coming in, Hollis?" Dante asked with an edge in his voice. He didn't like to be kept waiting.

"Sorry, Father. Sunny stopped me," she offered as an excuse, the only excuse she would ever use, and the only one he would allow. He gave her a sharp nod.

"Come sit. I'm waiting on Nala and Rachel. And here they are now."

Hollis turned to find the two other hunters walk through the door. They sauntered in, their heads high and chins jutted out, proud to have been summoned. They were both exceptional hunters in their own rights, but Hollis was better. Their presence caused her to wonder why he wanted to see all three of them. Perhaps he had another mission for them, though they had each been out on a witch hunt last night.

"Take your seats," Dante directed as he stood, straightening his suit and refastening the bottom button. In his suits, he appeared dapper and put together like Pierce Brosnan in a James Bond movie, even down to the silver streaking his otherwise black sideburns. "It has recently come to my attention through a reliable source—"

"You mean snitch," Rachel sarcastically snickered.

Dante inclined his head. "Such a crass term. I prefer 'source.' Anyway, this source confirmed what a separate source had previously supplied. The town we have been looking for is, in fact, in Colorado. It is called Havenwood Falls."

"Weren't we just in Colorado, like a year ago?" Nala impatiently asked. She had been one of the main hunters first tailing, then keeping watch, on Macy Blackstone when she had inadvertently stumbled upon them.

"Indeed, but my memory of it has remained maddeningly elusive. No doubt a side effect of those damned witches the *other* Blackstones associate with."

"They shouldn't be allowed to use the name Blackstone," Rachel spat with disgust. Nala and Hollis both agreed.

"No, no. They are of our blood. Though they are misguided, we can bring them back into the fold, into our family, and redirect their purpose—help them see the error of their ways, so to speak," Dante clarified, looking each girl in the eye to ensure they understood.

"Do you know where in Colorado?" Hollis cut to the chase.

"No. That is the frustrating part. However, we know it is somewhere in the middle of the state. Most likely somewhere with a significant area of land where they could hide an entire town."

"How do we know your 'sources' aren't sending us on a wild goose chase?" Nala asked as she whipped her long blond hair behind her shoulder.

Dante sneered, and an evil glint entered his eyes. "I extracted the information from the witch myself. She couldn't help but tell me."

Nala and Rachel each swallowed hard. They knew what kind of

methods the source would have had to endure for Dante to get the information he wanted. Hollis didn't flinch. She knew he did what he had to, to get what he needed.

"Well, it's about damn time. When do we go?" Rachel asked, readjusting in her seat as if she wasn't afraid of Dante's tactics. They all feared him. The ones like Hollis had the ability to hide their fear, which separated them from the others.

"No." Dante surveyed the girls slowly, taking measure of something they weren't aware of. "For this mission, I need to be able to completely trust the person I send. She would have to be able to go undercover, be skilled at listening, and have the ability to not act on instinct—to conceal her hunter side for the greater good. For this mission, I choose Hollis. She is the best suited."

Without reaction, Hollis simply nodded her acceptance. The other girls groaned.

"Then why are we here?" Rachel asked. She had a tendency to speak out of turn. Dante put up with it to a point. He had reached that point. The look he gave her had her shrinking back into her seat. Hollis couldn't help the glow of approval she kept hidden in her chest. Rachel got on her nerves the most.

"*That* is exactly why I chose her. Hollis can control her reactions and simply observe. Also, not to mention, Macy has seen you both and most likely would recognize you right away. She never met Hollis during her stay, as Hollis was out on an extended mission." Hollis realized he had called the other girls in to teach them a lesson and to, once more, instill competition amongst them by elevating one over the other. She didn't agree with his tactics for camaraderie amongst teams, but he did get results. He turned and looked to her. "Will you go, daughter?"

"Of course, Father. When should I be ready to leave for Colorado?"

"Tomorrow morning. I will have Grace get flights prepared. Pack light. Disguise yourself. I want you to blend in. Be a tourist, if need be. I want specific information on the town and certain people within it. I'll get a list together while you pack."

Hollis inclined her head in a half nod and half bow, ready to serve.

"How are you so sure she'll find it based on 'somewhere in the middle of Colorado'?" Nala asked, but Hollis could hear the tinge of jealousy behind her tone.

"Can you find it, Hollis?" Dante pointedly asked.

"I won't come home until I do."

Dante smiled. "That's my girl."

And that was how Hollis found herself at the private airport in Grand Junction, waiting for a shuttle to take her to Montrose, yet another small city in the middle of the Colorado mountains.

CHAPTER 2

*H*ollis searched the small cities and towns of Colorado for over a month with nothing to show for her work. Until one afternoon, in the middle of May, she found herself wandering the small town of Durango. About to give up her search for the day, she overheard a middle-aged couple talking in aggravated hushed tones.

"We'll miss the bus up the mountain," the woman huffed with her hands on her hips, clearly frustrated with the man beside her. She shot a reproachful gaze at him.

"Don't get in a tizzy. We'll make it just fine," the man attempted to placate her.

"A *tizzy*? The special instructions we were given by the Havenwood Falls Tourism Bureau said the bus doesn't wait for anyone. It'll be your fault if we miss it," she rebutted with a harsh whisper. The woman cast eyes full of blame on the man, obviously willing him to feel her subtle wrath.

Hollis, excited about the potential lead, stayed several strides behind them, but continued to follow. She had very little in the way of clothes with her, but she always took everything in her small backpack every time she left the motel room in anticipation of an occasion such as this one. She never knew when luck would strike, and she would need to follow a lead.

Hollis continued to follow the couple behind a truck stop. Sure enough, a small bus, more like a shuttle, had its front doors open and passengers loading into it. Hollis had never seen a bus completely wrapped with images such as the beautiful scenery of trees and mountains as this one did. The imagery evolved from one season to the next: winter to spring to summer and then to fall around the outside. But no words indicated where the bus was headed. Hollis wondered how anyone would know this bus went to their destination. She might never have found it had she not been following the couple who obviously knew where they were headed. Hollis moved in close and casually examined the shuttle while awaiting her turn to board.

Out of the corner of her eye, the words *Havenwood Falls* shimmered as if by magic across the side of the bus. Hollis knew witches were involved, so it most likely was magic, but either way she had to admit it was a cool effect.

"Miss, will you be joining us on our journey up the mountain today?" the shuttle driver asked, breaking Hollis out of her entrancement. She cleared her throat.

"Yes. Yes, I will."

"Well, come on then." He waved her on and looked at his watch. "It's about time to be on the road before dark. The roads get mighty difficult in the best of times, but at night they can be a mite treacherous."

At Hollis's frown, the little man supplied a hearty laugh. "But I know my way around these parts like the back of my hand."

He examined the back of his hands, then winked at her. He moved inside the shuttle and to his seat, allowing her to climb aboard.

Hollis found an empty bench a couple rows from the front. Quickly, she surveyed the impeccable inside of the shuttle, located the emergency exit windows, and noted the couple who joined right before her and the three others previously seated. Everyone seemed to mind their own business except for one man in the back who eyed her suspiciously. She took the seat next to the window and tossed her backpack on the seat beside her, preventing anyone from taking it. Tugging at the collar of her new striped button-down shirt while simultaneously attempting not to retch at the sight of her bright white tennis shoes, she lamented the tourist look she had donned for the sake of the mission. Hollis sighed and hoped all her efforts would be worth it in the end. The shuttle waited another minute, then the driver closed the doors and started the engine.

"Buckle up!" the driver announced. "These roads have their twists and turns. Wouldn't want you falling out of your seat and giving the town another meaning to its name—Havenwood *Falls*." He chuckled, finding himself and his cheesy joke humorous, and pulled out of the lot. After several minutes of silence, the driver shouted, looking into the rearview mirror, startling several of the riders.

"Just a couple of announcements I've been asked to give." He cleared his throat as if reciting from memory. "If you're returning home, then welcome back. If you are here for the local fun, May 25, the annual Moons in the Mist Bonfire will be happening in Danzan Park by the lake. We have a farmers market every Saturday morning in Cook's Corner Park, First Friday Art Walk in the square, Second Saturday Movies in the Park also in Danzan Park, and Third Thursday Music in the Square. There is always something fun going on in Havenwood Falls!"

"Small towns . . . how quaint," Hollis muttered under her breath. She sat back and thought over how boring life must be in such a small, secluded place to have so many events. Once the bus ascended through the trees, the road curved back and forth. The monotony of the forest scenery, the hum of the shuttle engine, and the rocking with every curve eventually lulled Hollis to sleep. But just before her eyes closed, she saw the glow of several pairs of eyes peering out from the now darkened forest. Then she drifted into peaceful nothing.

9

"Welcome to Havenwood Falls!" the driver shouted, startling Hollis awake.

"I can't believe I fell asleep," she whispered with near panic as she looked around, taking stock of her possessions and her surroundings. She couldn't believe she let her guard down in such a way. Never before had she fallen asleep in public—on a job, no less. The false security of the bus ride shocked her to a fully awakened state. The bus passed a large sign made of layered stone and metalwork complete with a spotlight, welcoming them to the town of Havenwood Falls. The road crested a ridge and finally opened up to reveal a fantasy hidden amidst the mountains, a small world lighting the darkening sky. Hollis couldn't help but absorb everything on a first impression basis. She could understand why people might want to visit a small town like this quaint postcard-esque oasis, but not her. She preferred the anonymity a larger city provided. It's harder to stealthily move about when your neighbors watch your every move, or when the town's gossip shares your private moments.

No, a small town was not for her.

Yet something undeniably alluring was at work within Havenwood Falls. The draw had to be part of the magic—she just didn't know if it was witch-made or natural.

"All right, folks, I'll be pulling in at Whisper Falls Inn. If you have reservations or need somewhere to stay, I highly recommend this inn. However, there are a few other options for lodging if Whisper Falls doesn't suit you. If you want to be dropped off elsewhere, let me know and stay in the shuttle."

Hollis followed a guy off the bus. The sound of Whisper Falls Inn was appealing—not to mention close—and Hollis figured she'd make first contact and learn more about the town in the morning.

She acknowledged the driver and offered him a tip. When her hand touched his, something sparked in his eyes. Not romantic, but more . . . *other*.

"You may find your stay has more to offer than you planned on. Enjoy Havenwood Falls, miss."

And with his random words and the slightly creepy encounter,

Hollis tightly smiled and then proceeded to practically run into the guy who had stared at her on the bus and who continued to do so. His eyes perused her person from head to toe, and he cocked his head as if deciding something, then darted without a trace into the town square.

"Creepy! What are they drinking in the water here?" she said under her breath, shaking off the effects of the weirdo, then followed the same couple she had trailed onto the bus up the steps of the nicely refurbished three-story Victorian manor. The inn looked straight out of the 1800s, complete with a charming wraparound porch, tall turrets, and beautifully painted gingerbread trim. She followed the couple all the way in, through the lobby area to the front desk, tugging at her shirt positioned just right to cover most of the ink on her shoulders and adjusting the plain straight-legged jeans she would never choose to wear.

"Welcome to Havenwood Falls and Whisper Falls Inn," a teenage girl said. "Are you checking in with a reservation tonight?" she professionally asked the couple in front of her.

While Hollis waited her turn, she admired the inn's original woodwork and decor while she stretched out her witch hunter senses, but she didn't pick up any witches or other hunters in the inn. She relaxed. At least there was that. Perhaps the inn was a place she could hide in peace while she staked out the town.

"Hi! I'm Aurelia Petran. How can I help you? Do you have a reservation with us?" the girl at the desk asked Hollis with a partial smile. She was a little on the thin side with medium-dark brown hair and large brown eyes.

"No, I don't have one. I have cash if you have a room available for tonight. Or if not, could you point me to another place?"

"No, no, don't go anywhere else. We have a room available. Do you have a preference of view—perhaps the town square?"

Hollis didn't have to think about it. "Yes, the town square." She hesitated, then remembered she had a part to play and added, "Please."

"This your first time in Havenwood Falls, then?" the teen pried.

"It is."

The young girl bit her lip when it was obvious Hollis wasn't going to give her much more, then rolled her eyes.

"Your name?" she asked, then snarkily tacked on, "please." Obviously not missing Hollis's awkward response.

"Why?" Hollis suspiciously asked.

The girl frowned and pointed at the computer. "For your reservation. I need to know what name to put it under."

Not wanting to draw more attention to herself, Hollis complied. "Hollis."

Aurelia narrowed her eyes for a moment before proceeding. "And your last name?"

"Blacks—" She stopped herself. Man, something about this town had her off her covert game. "Black. Hollis Black."

The girl lifted a skeptical brow. "Okay then, Hollis Black. Here is your key. Second floor, up those stairs." She pointed over Hollis's shoulder, across the lobby to the grand staircase, and smiled with a lot of attitude and teenage angst.

"Thank you."

"Hey, guys!" Aurelia greeted someone behind Hollis. "Nice timing. You missed the shuttle drop-off." The young girl rolled her eyes again then shrugged. "But never fear, I was here and checked everybody in," she sarcastically told the two newcomers who entered the room from the other side of the inn.

"Sorry, Aurelia, but we needed to help"—the woman shot a quick look to the man next to her before continuing—"Mammie in the kitchen."

"Meet our newest guest." Aurelia gestured toward Hollis who was quietly padding up the steps already, hoping to avoid small talk with the hotel locals. "This is Hollis Black. She's going to stay with us tonight."

"Hello, Hollis, welcome to our inn. I'm Michaela, the owner, and you met my sister. This is Xandru, my fiancé." She sighed when she looked over at the large handsome man who playfully grabbed Michaela around the waist and pulled her back against his chest.

"My permanent fiancé, it seems. Maybe someday I'll be able to call you husband," she privately grumbled to him.

"Hello," Hollis said as the extent of her pleasantries, awkward with the new turn of events.

"Do you know how long you plan on staying?" Michaela asked while she swatted away advances from Xandru so she could talk. He clearly had other things on his mind than stopping to chat with a new guest.

"I'm not sure yet. Perhaps a few days."

"Oh, you must stay at least through the weekend for the big town bonfire. It's so much fun!" The young girl practically bounced with excitement.

"Maybe I can. I look forward to seeing your town tomorrow in daylight."

"Well, let us know if you need anything while you're here," Xandru added, more distracted with Michaela.

"Goodnight, Hollis," Michaela added as she turned to Xandru and kissed his chin.

"Goodnight." Hollis quickly moved up the steps before anyone could ask her anything else. Though they seemed friendly enough, she had no idea if they were anything supernatural—as their strange greenish-gray eye color seemed to indicate—or simply human pawns in the witch's world in Havenwood Falls. Her gift only allowed her to discern witches, their magic, and other witch hunters. Something about watching the two relate stirred a longing she hadn't felt in a long time.

"Just another reason to not stay longer than necessary," Hollis whispered. She resolved to find other lodging sites and keep moving after a day or two so no one got to know her or her business.

CHAPTER 3

The morning light streaked through the window as Hollis covered her head with the blankets, groaned, and turned away.

"Shit, could it be any brighter here? It's going to be one of those days. I can already tell." Stretching, she realized she slept all night for the first time in . . . well, she couldn't remember when. Often the hunters had evening drills, or she simply couldn't sleep. Rolling out of bed, she grumbled expletives as she got dressed.

Once the initial shock of morning wore off, Hollis quietly snuck down the staircase, hoping to leave unnoticed, in search of coffee.

"Morning, Hollis!" a chipper female voice called out.

She turned to the counter to see not Michaela but a tall beautiful redhead with the palest skin and blue eyes.

"Morning," she replied with less enthusiasm. "I don't think I met you last night." Hollis wasn't even sure why she cared to try. She wouldn't be in Havenwood Falls long.

"I'm Sindi Scott. I work the morning shift. Michaela is probably still in bed. Coffee?"

"Mind reader?" Hollis asked with a playful smile, yet her eyebrow lifted in silent question.

Sindi cocked her head and looked at Hollis strangely, like she wasn't sure if she was truly asking or not. Only in Havenwood Falls apparently would someone not consider that a cheesy joke.

Apparently Sindi decided Hollis was joking and offered a smile. "Nope, just have worn that same expression myself plenty of days."

"Where would I find some? Coffee, that is."

"There is breakfast and beverages in the dining room," Sindi answered, pointing in the opposite direction. "Or straight out the door and about half a block west is Coffee Haven, which is usually the more bustling café. But if you're looking for quiet, there's also Broastful Brew. It's on the opposite side of the square from here. Just cut across the square diagonally and you'll find it."

"Coffee Haven it is. Thanks," Hollis said and offered a slight smile. She didn't want to come off as too rude; that would draw a different type of attention. Her goal today: blend in. Thus the need for wearing plain jeans, a black plain T-shirt, her long unruly dark hair up in a ponytail, and boring gray tennis shoes. She didn't do tennis shoes. It was only to play the tourist role her father chose for her, that she wore them.

"I wouldn't have pegged you as a sneakers kinda girl," Sindi randomly offered. Her comment caught Hollis off guard.

"Excuse me?" Hollis asked, looking down at her new tennis shoes—she had even attempted to scuff them up to look worn.

Sindi shrugged. "You just struck me as a shit-kicker or boots with buckles kinda girl. No offense."

"None taken." Hollis smirked, then turned to go. Observant girl. She'd need to remember that. Moving to another inn might need to be in her near future.

Hollis jogged down the front steps and paused, taking in the scene before her. The town literally surrounded a big square, the center being green like a park, complete with walking paths and a fountain. Connected buildings filled with businesses and restaurants ran along each side of the square except for the north end. There stood a large official-looking brick building with a clock tower—had to be City Hall—and the local police station resided adjacent to it.

"The square can wait for coffee," she muttered to herself.

"Everything can wait for coffee." The male voice came out of nowhere from her left. She hadn't even heard him approach and frowned at the distracting effect the town so quickly had on her.

Hollis gave him a curt smile and a nod. "True."

"You must be new here. You look lost, plus you're coming out of the inn." The nosy man had the audacity to approach her.

Do people in small towns not mind their own business? Hollis wondered to herself.

"Are you headed into Coffee Haven? I can show you the way. I was headed there myself." The man gave her a big toothy grin highlighting his pearly whites. His hands stayed in his pockets, apparently trying to make himself appear smaller and nonthreatening. Hollis had studied people and their mannerisms; she could read most people with ease. This one wasn't creepy, just overly friendly. Plus Hollis could handle herself in a fight if she needed to fend him off for any reason.

"You're a lot to take in, aren't you?" Hollis raised an eyebrow. About to brush him off, she couldn't help but notice that the nosy man was a big piece of gorgeous man-meat—olive skin, defined muscles, dark hair, and dark gray eyes. She also couldn't miss the low-frequency vibration that emanated from him. Witch. Or at least half witch and half something else. His frequency caused her to think of Grace back home; hers was similar.

"I've been told that before. I'm Ryne Calloway. And you are . . . ?" He let the end of his word hang in the air, waiting for her to respond.

"A stranger. Didn't your mama tell you not to talk to strangers, Ryne Calloway?" Hollis turned to leave, but not before catching the brief pain that registered on his face. The look was gone almost the instant it had occurred. Hollis wondered what pain he endured.

"If you told me your name, you wouldn't be a stranger, now would you?" He moved along next to her and smiled confidently, knowing his line was cheesy. He had an endearing quality about him. Hollis knew better but decided to make nice in Havenwood Falls. If nothing else, she might get some information out of him.

"Hollis Black." She smiled, then kept trying to walk away.

"Wait! Where you goin', Hollis Black?" Ryne moved to catch up to her, and with his long strides, it didn't take him long.

"Coffee." She pointed toward the shop with the sign that read *Coffee Haven* on the outside, while simultaneously glancing in the window of a fun-looking vintage clothing shop called Callie's Consignments. She told herself to duck in there later as her wardrobe now seriously lacked.

"Right. Do you mind if I tag along? I don't have to sit with you. I was headed there anyway when I saw you standing in front of the inn looking lost and in need of a guide."

"I'm not lost." Hollis glared at him.

"Not anymore, because I'm here to show you around." He smiled again, unfazed by her attitude.

"No thanks."

"Why not?" Ryne's expression softened, and he took on a puppy-dog-like quality in his pout.

"First of all, I don't know you. Second, I like to be alone. Third, don't you have a job or somewhere to be?" Hollis ticked off her reasons with her fingers.

"You do know me—we just met. Alone is so boring. And yes, I do have a job, but I have today off." He, too, ticked off his responses with his fingers. "So I can be your personal tour guide and show you all the cool places around town."

Suddenly what he said made sense to Hollis. And why not? "Okay. It would be helpful to have someone show me around and tell me about the people—the town, I mean."

"But first coffee?" he asked, his face lit up like a kid at Christmas.

"Right." She gave him a funny look. Was he for real?

He opened the door for her, and the fresh smell of coffee beans rushed out, assaulting her senses, shocking her into a fully awakened state. "Mmmm."

Ryne indicated Hollis should order her coffee first, then he sneakily interjected himself and ordered his drink as well, his wallet already out and ready to pay the bill.

"Can I interest you in today's scone? There aren't too many left," the girl behind the counter said with a wide smile. She took Hollis off guard with her silvery-blond hair and her bright turquoise eyes. She tried not to stare, but the woman was beyond intriguing.

"Morning, Willow! We'll take two please." Ryne turned to Hollis. "Her scones are the best ever."

"Here you go, Ryne. The coffees will be ready in just a moment." Willow turned to Hollis and stared at her a second longer than necessary, almost as if she'd slipped into a trance, then smiled. "Stick with this guy. He'll show you what our little town is all about. Have fun!"

Hollis, slightly unsettled by the barista's words, followed Ryne to an open table for two near the wall in the middle of the shop.

"Who was that?" Hollis inclined her head in Willow's direction.

"That is Willow Fairchild. She owns the joint and bakes the best scones—did I already mention that?" Ryne set their coffees down, winked at her, and pulled out a chair for Hollis, which she looked at, dumbfounded. "It's a chair. You sit in it."

Snapping out of her haze, she frowned and sat abruptly. "I know what a fucking chair is. I've never had anyone pull one out for me before."

Ryne was silent for a moment, then with a puzzled look, added, "Really? Not even on a date?"

"I don't date much. I'm busy with"—she hesitated, looking for the right words—"education and work."

"Oh, you're one of those types."

She frowned. "One of what types?"

"Focused. Motivated. Studious . . . that type." Ryne shrugged, leaned back, and stretched out his legs, crossing them at the ankles.

Taken aback, Hollis had never thought about the "type" she might be, but those were as good as any. She shrugged and reached for her coffee and the plate with the blueberry scone on it. "Thank you."

"You have to try your scone," Ryne said around a mouthful of his own. His eyes practically rolled back into his head with sheer ecstasy. "Like right now."

Hollis couldn't help but laugh. Right there in public it looked like the man she shared a table with was having a private moment with a pastry.

"Would you and your scone like a room?"

But it was too late. Ryne had shoved the entire scone into his mouth and smiled a big crumbly smile full of blueberries and flaky goodness. Still he nodded and raised his eyebrows suggestively.

Hollis snorted and practically choked on her coffee. She had never made such a sound before. Slightly embarrassed, she righted herself and took a bite of her scone.

She nearly groaned herself, now understanding. "You're right. This is the best scone."

"You don't laugh much, do you?" Ryne asked, suddenly serious as he watched her eat her small controlled bite.

She cleared her throat and turned to observe the customers of the café. Other than coffee, observation was, in fact, why she now sat at Coffee Haven.

"Tell me about the town," she prompted him as she took another bite.

Ryne leaned back in his chair and crossed an ankle over his opposite knee. "What would you like to know?"

"How big is it? What do people do here? Why is it way up in these mountains? Who's in charge?" She shrugged around another bite. "You pick."

"Well, all right. I'm not originally from here. I've only lived here about a year, so I'll do my best to answer your questions. We get a lot of tourists, especially during the winter for our great skiing, but we also have a lot of town events that many out-of-towners find fun to participate in." Ryne sipped his coffee. "Let's see . . . Why is it in the mountains? From the stories I've heard, the founding families— the original townspeople—were looking for a quiet secluded place to settle down in the late 1800s, and this is where they ended up."

"Who's in charge? Do you have like a government or elected officials?" Hollis asked, absorbing all he said.

Ryne shrugged. "Mayor, city council, sheriff . . ." He paused in mid-sentence. "You know, all the typical stuff . . ." He quickly took another sip of coffee.

Hollis noted his pause, as if he wanted to say more but stopped himself. She wondered about the secrecy of the town and how it all worked. What would he do if she outright asked? Did he even know he was part witch? Would she scare him off if she were to be so blunt? She'd consider asking, but not today.

"So what do you do for work?"

Ryne almost looked relieved when she moved on to something else. "I work construction with McCabe & Sons Construction and a little bit at the ski lift this past winter."

"What else do you do?" Hollis kept him talking not because she was interested in him or what he did, but because she was able to listen to more around the room when she didn't have to talk. However, something about the ring of his voice, the low timbre of it, drew her in, and she found she wanted him to keep talking.

Suddenly Ryne's voice faded into the background as her senses kicked in, alerting her to not only one witch's presence, but two. She watched out of the corner of her eye as a woman perhaps in her forties walked in with a teenage girl and happily chatted with Willow and another girl at the counter. Both of the newcomers registered to her as witches.

"Have Gallad and Macy set a wedding date yet?" Willow asked the woman with a smile.

Macy? Macy Blackstone? Hollis completely tuned in.

"Not yet. They've decided to move slow. Which I, for one, am pleased with. I adore Macy, but I think they're still young and more time isn't going to hurt them," the woman said matter-of-factly.

"Well, you are Gallad's mom. You're entitled to think that. Do the Blackstones agree?" Willow's question confirmed they did indeed speak of Macy Blackstone.

"Oh yes, Lilith and I seem to be on the same page. And I think the kids are, too, now that hormones have settled down." The woman with long curly dark hair flippantly gestured with her hand at Willow, clearly not embarrassed.

"Oh, Mom, really!" The teenager with the same curly dark hair rolled her eyes, clearly embarrassed.

"Ronya, you're terrible," Willow said with a wink, and handed them their drinks in to-go cups.

"I have to take this one to the dentist, or we'd stay for a bit," the woman named Ronya explained.

"We'll see you soon! Bye, Ronya. Good luck at the dentist, Gianna." Willow waved and welcomed the next customer.

Hollis tuned back to Ryne just as he was saying something about the bonfire party.

"Will you be staying for it? It's this Saturday. I haven't been, but heard it's pretty epic."

"The bonfire?" Hollis clarified. At his nod, she continued, "I was thinking about it. Can tourists just show up?"

"Of course! You can go with me, then you won't be a tourist." He smiled at her and took a big gulp, draining the last of his mug.

"Where to next?" Hollis looked at him with a question in her eyes.

"A pretty tourist such as yourself needs an experienced guide to show her around so as not to be taken advantage of by the local riffraff. And I have volunteered myself to give you my time today." He placed his hand over his chest and bowed his head. "Out of the goodness of my heart and concern for your well-being, of course."

"Wow, that's so generous of you," Hollis began with sarcasm. "But I'm good. Thank you for the coffee and amazing scone, but I am fine on my own."

"I bet you are, but do you have fun on your own? Just a thought," Ryne said with a raised eyebrow. He returned his mug to the counter and strolled out the door.

"Did he really just leave me sitting here?" Hollis sat stunned with her mouth open and her gaze toward the door.

"Honey, if you don't recognize a keeper when one is right in front of your face, you don't deserve him." A tiny and frail-looking elderly woman at the table next to her offered her opinion without guilt or shame. Clearly one of the town's busybodies, Hollis noted.

"Oh, Irene, don't scare off the new girl," Willow whispered from the table she was cleaning nearby. "Enjoy your day, Hollis." Willow went back to the table she was bussing, Irene went back to her breakfast, and Hollis stood up with nothing else to do but leave.

CHAPTER 4

"You don't scare easily, do you?" Hollis asked with an eyebrow raised, her stance widened and her arms crossed over her chest. A very cool and collected Ryne leaned against a vintage streetlamp, waiting for her.

"You're not as scary as you think you are," he replied as he pushed himself off the lamp and moved toward her. "Plus, you didn't think I would give up my new tour guide gig that quick did you?"

"Well . . ."

"Come on, you want to see the town, don't you?" Ryne held out his hand.

"I'm not taking your hand. I just met you." Hollis kept her arms crossed and strode by him, heading straight for a shop with a peculiar name. She cocked her head and peered up at the sign. "Does that really say *Hey, Nice Glass*?"

"Sure does. There's a lot of shops and some restaurants. We've got Backwoods for outdoor wear and equipment, and even a wine-tasting storefront for the vineyard at the edge of town. Anywhere you want to go in particular?" Ryne asked, strolling along beside her as if he had nowhere better to be.

"The vineyard sounds cool. What's that like?" Hollis asked, curious if it could perhaps be associated with the Blackstones. Her father had told her stories of his youth back in the mid-1800s and his family's tobacco farm and vineyard—it wouldn't be much of a leap to think the Blackstones of Havenwood Falls would start something similar. She tipped her head up, closed her eyes for a second, and simply enjoyed the feel of the warm May sunshine on her face. The sounds of water splashing from the fountain at the center of the square offered her a brief sensation of peace.

"The Stone Falls Winery. It's a small vineyard owned by a family named the Blackstones. There's also some cabins called NamaStays Inn on the property, and they do yoga or some shit like that." Ryne clapped his hand over his mouth like he forgot he was trying to impress a lady and be on his best behavior. Hollis almost choked on a laugh.

"Interesting. And you said they have a storefront here in the square too?" She had been right, but remained casual.

"It's called Soothing Sips, and it's just a little farther." He pointed ahead of them.

Hollis suddenly stopped. She hadn't sensed the presence of another hunter nearby. Though she was still a slight distance away, she would have. Ryne gave her a quizzical expression.

"I just remembered I wanted to go into Callie's Consignment after coffee and look for clothes. It's back that way, right?" She pointed behind them. Most likely none of the Blackstones were present at Soothing Sips, but she couldn't risk their sudden appearance. The last people she needed to see right now or even get close to were the Blackstones. They would recognize her as a fellow hunter, and her mission would be over before it even began.

"Well yeah, but there's more to see this way." He thumbed behind him as he faced her. "We can make our way back around," Ryne suggested.

"New plan," Hollis countered. "I want to walk through the park. We don't need to walk by—what is that? City Hall?" She pointed to the larger buildings at the north end of the square.

"Yeah, the big one in the middle is City Hall. The police station and the chamber of commerce on either sides." He inhaled, then shrugged. "Sure, we could do that." Ryne's face lit up with a genuine smile, completely content. They cut across the street and entered the beautiful park-like setting at one of the paved, bench-lined walkways leading toward the fountain in the middle.

Hollis and Ryne spent the next couple hours walking in and out of several shops. Hollis chose to skip Howe's Herbal Shoppe with the excuse she had allergies to a lot of plants, but truthfully she could feel several powerful witches inside, and her skin practically crawled with the tingling sensation up and down her arms—her hunter instincts alerting her. Inside Backwoods Sport & Ski, she purchased hiking boots, claiming she wanted to hike the trails to the falls the next day. After circling back around, she found herself genuinely excited to visit Callie's Consignments.

"Hey, thank you for the tour, but I'd like to hit this next shop on my own. You know, try on clothes, take my time. I'd rather not put on a show." She shrugged sheepishly, pretending to be shy all of a sudden.

Ryne actually blushed and stammered. "Oh, of course. I didn't mean to overstep my boundaries. It's been fun showing you around. I like to remember all the things I came to love about this town when I moved here."

Hollis studied his face and noticed the minute lines of tension around his eyes that hadn't been there all day, and the essence that made him witch flared at his sudden unease. "Ryne, how did you come to move here?"

He shifted on his feet, suddenly uncomfortable. "Well, I came here with my mom about a year ago. She loves it here. We had to . . . She needed a new start, and I felt responsible for her after my dad died. I couldn't just let her go off to a new place alone. We ended up here." He shrugged. "That's it. Pretty simple."

But Hollis had the feeling it was anything but simple. It wasn't her business. And she didn't want to get involved. So why was she even asking?

"Cool."

He seemed relieved she didn't press for more information. Which, of course, made her want to press further. But not now.

"Hey! Would you like to meet up for lunch after you're done shopping?" he asked, like he'd had the greatest idea.

"Why?" She suspiciously narrowed her eyes and cocked her head.

"Because I enjoyed spending time with you; you're new and don't know anyone; and everybody's got to eat, right?" He was grasping at straws. Hollis might've found it cute under other circumstances. But she was on a mission to reveal all the witches of Havenwood Falls, not go on a date with one.

"I don't think so. Thanks, though," she responded, suddenly wanting to soften the blow for him.

He scrunched his face. "Okay, then how about dinner? I could show you the town at night. We have some nice places to eat. Plus I think it's the third Thursday tonight, so there should be live music in the square." His eyes lit up with remembrance of the local event. She couldn't deny that.

"All right. Dinner. I'll be ready at the inn. Six?" Her arms crossed over her chest suggested she wasn't too happy about it, but deep inside, if she was honest with herself, an excitement bubbled at the prospect of the personal attention and the possibility of fun.

Ryne smiled from ear to ear. He mock bowed and backed away. "Until then, my lady."

Hollis smirked at his silly antics. Why was this playful guy even remotely interested in her? Granted, she wasn't half bad in appearance—she had used her looks in her favor a time or two on a hunt—but she wasn't even trying. In fact, she was doing the opposite of trying—she had been trying to get rid of him most of the morning. He just wouldn't take no for an answer. Hollis chuckled to herself, then opened the door into the vintage wonderland that was Callie's Consignments and unexpectedly got hit with a wave of toxicity that almost had her doubling over.

A young woman rushed past her and out the door, taking the

toxic magic stench with her. Hollis had encountered that feeling too many times to mistake it for anything else.

Black magic.

But who was the witch, and what was she doing here? Did the council in Havenwood Falls allow such behavior from their witches?

No. She shook herself out of the effects it had on her. Hollis didn't care if a witch practiced black magic in Havenwood Falls. That wasn't her purpose this time. Though everything within her wanted to go after the woman and punish her for her participation in the dark arts. It didn't matter who she was or why she did it. The witch deserved to die.

But what about a half witch? The unwelcome question floated through her mind.

One with warm, inviting gray eyes who made me feel things I didn't realize were a part of me? She had never questioned herself or her instincts before. What was it about this town that caused her to do so only one day in?

"You shopping or getting out of the sunshine?" a woman yelled from behind the counter. She was reminiscent of a young gypsy with a flowy top, colorful skirt, and enough bracelets to stock a store. The woman looked expectantly at Hollis with a wild eyes.

"You Callie?" Hollis ventured a guess.

The woman squinted at her with cynicism. "Maybe. Who wants to know?"

"Just a guess. I like your shop. I'm Hollis. I'm just visiting your town and need to pick up a few new things."

"These are not mere *things*. These"—Callie stretched her arms wide across her store with pride—"these are artwork, amazing vintage pieces of art."

Hollis cocked an eyebrow. She had never heard anyone speak of clothing in such a manner. As if it mattered. As if it could be a part of you, or rather an extension of you. "Got it. What would you show to me, without knowing me?"

Callie moved toward Hollis, pursed her lips, and frowned, taking

27

her in from head to toe—noting her tennis shoes with a cocked eyebrow of her own. "That's not your everyday look, is it?" But her question was really more of a statement, needing no answer. "Luckily for you, I like a challenge. Let's go find you, and not whomever this is wearing tennis shoes." She waved a hand in a circle in front of her, indicating all of Hollis. "Whatever suppressed thing you have going on is radiating off you, making me, and most likely the entire town, sick."

Hollis's eyes grew wide. Who did she just engage herself with? Not a witch—she would have felt that. But Callie was definitely something. Hollis wondered how many *somethings* other than witches could live in a small town.

"Don't look surprised. I'm good at reading people." Callie waved her off and shook her bangles. "Gypsy. Magical balls. Tarot cards. Fortune telling," she ticked off with a wink. But Hollis wasn't sure if Callie was telling her she was a real gypsy or if she portrayed the stereotype of one for fun.

"You definitely play the part well," Hollis returned.

"It's not a part. And you have a lot to learn, don't you?" Callie spun around and headed toward a rack of a variety of different types of "pieces," as she called them. "We'll start here."

After an hour or two, Hollis had tried on a multitude of clothes and had just put her uncomfortable "tourist clothes" back in place when she felt tingles like electricity shoot up her arms. Then she heard something that stopped her cold.

"Hey, Macy! Perfect timing. A new batch of vintage jewelry was delivered this week. I want to show you," Callie called out from across the room.

"Hi, Callie! I was hoping you would say that. I've been jonesing for . . ." She paused. "Something new," she said slowly, as if searching.

Hollis pulled back the dressing room fabric the tiniest bit to spy out. Sure enough, a girl just out of high school with white-blond hair and bright blue eyes matching the description her family had given her of Macy Blackstone stood in the center of the store, looking around with a confused expression.

"Macy? What the hell is wrong with you? Did you see a ghost?" Callie asked, half joking.

"Is anyone else here?" Macy whispered, moving closer to Callie. Callie frowned at her and nodded.

"There's a new girl in the dressing room," she whispered back. Hollis had a hard time hearing them, but by reading their lips she was able to make out most of what they said.

Macy frowned. Hollis knew Macy could sense a fellow hunter's presence just as Hollis could sense hers, but Macy wouldn't know Hollis was of her own kin.

"What? Is she dangerous?" Callie whispered, but didn't appear afraid.

Macy shrugged her shoulders. She leaned in and whispered something in Callie's ear, then backed up and said more loudly, "I'm sorry, I only have a few minutes, but I can come back to look later, too."

"Sure. The necklaces and bracelets are over here." Callie led Macy to the stands of jewelry. Macy did a quick perusal, then left the store.

Hollis breathed a sigh of relief and gathered the items she wanted to keep. She wasn't going to let a potential encounter with Macy take away from the fantastic new clothes—pieces—she found. Her father would be disappointed if he knew her train of thought preferred fashion over her mission. The absurdity of the thought almost made her laugh. She would still try to follow Macy; it was a win-win in her book. Good thing her father wasn't there.

She stepped out with her items and went to the counter. Callie paid attention to her, but didn't seem any different. She gathered the clothes from the counter and rang Hollis up with efficiency. The last item she handed to Hollis personally and happened to touch her hand.

"Thanks for your business." She paused, and her eyes quickly flashed as if she had a momentary blackout. Then as if nothing had happened, she smiled. "I hope you'll come back. If you ever want to take that leap, you'll fit in just fine. Maybe you'd even find it fun to come to a girls' night out sometime with me and my friends. You belong, Hollis. Especially now that you have cute shoes. I'd better not see those damn tennis sneakers again."

Hollis smiled shakily, slightly taken aback by Callie's bold intuitions. "Um, sure . . . okay, thanks." Hollis took the bag from Callie and gave her an odd look. "A gypsy, huh?"

Callie shrugged. "Gypsy," she replied. "You never know around here. See ya 'round!"

Hollis headed for the door with a lot more new things than clothes to consider.

Now to try to find Macy.

CHAPTER 5

*A*fter several minutes of searching for the direction Macy went, Hollis gave up and took her bag of new "pieces" back to her room at Whisper Falls Inn. On her way up the stairs, she was greeted by Michaela coming out of the parlor.

"Oh, hey, Hollis. How was your first day in Havenwood Falls?"

"It was . . . interesting. But I got some fun things at Callie's." Hollis held up her shopping bag.

"I love Callie. She's a good friend. Didn't you just love her store?" Michaela asked as she rounded the desk to take her position behind the computer. "Did she make you try on other shoes?"

"It was great. And, yeah, how did you know?" Hollis asked, looking down at the tennis shoes that made her skin itch with a desire to burn them.

"She has a thing against tennis shoes," Michaela said with a chuckle. "Especially if the person wearing them doesn't seem to fit them."

Hollis squinted. Did she really just say that? "What is with people and my shoes in this town?" she spat with frustrated irritation as she headed for the stairs.

"It's not your shoes, Hollis. It's what they're hiding," Michaela boldly stated as if she knew something.

"Whatever. I have a dinner thing to get ready for."

"A date? With Ryne? He's such a sweetheart. Don't break him, Hollis." Michaela approved and warned her all in one breath.

"Not a date. Just dinner. He doesn't take no for an answer." Hollis frowned. Too many people were keeping tabs on her already in this tiny town. Time to move.

"Oh, Michaela? Could you tell me which way to the vineyard? I thought I might like to see it and get some wine to take back with me."

"Of course. I'll draw you a map and have it sent up to your room."

"Thanks."

Hollis jogged the steps two at a time up to her room on the second floor, but just before she exited the stairwell, she overheard Michaela on the phone. "Hey, Addie, it's me. I have a guest by the name of Hollis Black. I think she's up to something or is more than she seems, if you know what I mean. I'll keep an eye out for the Court, but maybe you can check her out. She probably needs to register as a visitor." She paused. "Yeah, I think she's something other than . . . Just a hunch. Bye." She hung up the phone.

Hollis couldn't believe her ears. They'd discovered her faster than she thought. She didn't know who Addie was, but they were keeping their eyes on her.

They must have a way to keep track of supernaturals. I wonder how that works, Hollis questioned mentally with concern after she entered her room. Her jig might be up before she got much more than clothing.

Some time later, a folded map of the town slipped under her door. True to her word, Michaela circled the Stone Falls Winery and drew a path from the inn, making it an easy route to follow. Hollis knew it was a risk going somewhere the Blackstones were sure to be, but she wanted to see what she could find out, especially now the leash of her disguise grew shorter. Unfortunately, she didn't have time before dinner, but perhaps she could slip away after.

At six o'clock on the dot, Ryne pulled up in front of the inn, but

Hollis already waited outside for him. She didn't want him to come into the inn, knowing the town was full of busybodies. Earlier Hollis had decided to use her time with Ryne to her advantage and make it part of her cover: she had come to visit and spend time with her friend, Ryne.

"Well, don't you clean up nice?" Ryne smiled and started to reach out for her, then stopped himself, suddenly awkward.

To both their surprise, Hollis reached out in response to him and grabbed his hand. The smile that boy sported could have melted the hardest woman's heart. And if Hollis wasn't careful, she would be no exception.

"What can you show me tonight?" she asked, alleviating the awkward moment.

"We can eat on the square and enjoy the evening music by the gazebo—grab Napoli's pizza or something else close by." He pointed to where several townsfolk were setting up folding lawn chairs and spreading blankets on the grass, settling in for an evening of music. "Or we could go somewhere a little off the beaten path. There's a restaurant at the top of the falls—it's a little nicer but has a great view of the town—or we could . . ."

"Pizza. Napoli's sounds amazing. Not sure about the sitting around kumbaya-style with a bunch of strangers part."

"Pizza it is. We can eat inside and then decide on the music after we hear how it is. If it's a high school band practicing then . . ." He shrugged his shoulders and scrunched his face in distaste.

"Lead the way, then." She gestured for him to take the lead.

Napoli's was a nice family-run establishment. The inside boasted a darkened, cozy Italian flare. They found a table off to the side and away from a larger group of high school kids, probably headed out to hear the band. One boy in particular caught Hollis's eye. He looked about seventeen, lean and lanky with dark hair. The crowd he hung with looked about the same age and sported various skateboard gear. His bright blue eyes struck her. She had seen those eyes not only in the mirror, but on her father. If she tuned in to him, she could feel the energy of a fellow hunter, but just barely, as if he hadn't been awakened yet into his powers. Interesting. *He must be a Blackstone.* She had heard they slowed the awakening with Macy, too.

"Here it comes!" Ryne said with the excitement of a young boy.

Hollis watched with amusement. When he caught her looking, he didn't even blush.

"What? I love their pizza. It makes my mouth water just thinking about it." He pointed his fork at her. Hollis held her hands up in supplication. "You just wait. You are going to love it, too."

Hollis wasn't so sure, but his confidence in it alone made her want to try it.

An hour and an entire pizza later, Hollis and Ryne walked out of Napoli's. People of all ages now covered the green of town square. Music blared out into the four corners, and to Hollis's ear, the band didn't sound too bad. Children danced with each other and ran around while grandparents and older folk sat in folded chairs chatting and watching the young ones play. People listened, but most used it as a social opportunity. The sight was quaint and joyful, and the warmth of the moment caught Hollis off guard. She didn't see witches and witch hunters, vampires and werewolves, or any other supernatural race who might be hiding out in this small town. She simply saw people being people, and she found that refreshing.

"Would you like to find a seat and listen to the music? They don't sound half bad," Ryne said, slightly impressed.

"Actually, I was thinking I'd like to see the Stone Falls Winery and enjoy a glass of wine. Would you like to join me?" she asked hesitantly, as if she had never asked anyone out.

Ryne smiled and gave her a single nod. "That sounds like the perfect end to a perfect day."

"Are you always this cheesy?" Hollis asked.

Ryne feigned shock. "I'm hurt. I am not cheesy." He gently nudged her, but Hollis staggered under his strength. She had to fight her instinct to shove him back and realized he was playing with her. "But in all seriousness, I had a nice time today. You are a breath of fresh air in this town. And there is just something about you that draws me in," he said honestly.

"Really?" Hollis asked with confusion. She had never been described as a breath of fresh anything. And thinking over the day, she hadn't even been that nice to the guy. "I . . . I don't know what to say. Thank you?" she guessed.

Ryne laughed out loud. "That'll do."

He reached for her hand, and she let him take it as they walked up one side of the square, past the storefronts, and strolled into a residential part of the town she hadn't yet seen.

Hollis ignored the constant tingling she felt race up her arm at his contact, but considering he was only half witch, the sensation seemed dulled.

"The vineyard is through a neighborhood?" Hollis asked, taking in all the different types of houses.

"It's just up this road a few blocks, at the base of Mt. Alexa." Ryne pointed straight ahead of them. "See, just there you can see the white lights from the patio."

"That's pretty," Hollis caught herself saying. She frowned, then closed her mouth, confused at her own treacherous reactions.

"Sure is. The Blackstones are real nice people, and they've got a nice place here. Granted, I've only been here a few times, but I've enjoyed it every time."

Hollis considered what he said. "Would you say they are friends of yours?"

"We're not that close, but I've hung out some with their oldest son, Brock. And I know Gallad Augustine—he's engaged to their daughter Macy. They're a nice couple, though a bit unorthodox." Ryne frowned as if he wished he hadn't said that last part.

"What do you mean, unorthodox?" Hollis wasn't about to let it go.

"Well . . . I just mean . . . he's . . . and she's . . ." Ryne looked pained. "They're still young is all."

"Oh, I'm sure if they've got family and friends like you, they'll be in good hands." She decided to throw him a bone. He was obviously not used to hiding things.

His shoulders relaxed. "Oh look, they've got a fire going in the back. Let's head to the back patio."

Hollis looked up. The mountain towered above, a formidable shadow, reflecting what little daylight remained in combination with the glare from the town lights. Humbled and small was how she felt in its presence.

"Pretty amazing, isn't it?" Ryne asked, coming back to where she stood in awe. "It never gets old, looking at it."

"I have never seen anything quite as magical, and I've seen a lot," she admitted.

Lowering her gaze, she observed the vineyard establishment. The main building was a mixture of dark wood, clean lines, and a rustic modern vibe. Aspens dotted the landscape as well as large barrels of potted florals with trailing greenery. Small lanterns guided their steps from the graveled parking area up to the main walkway, leading them around to the back of the building where a concrete patio was brought to life with overhanging white lightbulbs and simple wooden table-and-chair sets. Modern garage doors opened into what appeared to be the main tasting area. But out past the patio was the vineyard—rows and rows of meticulously lined grape vines of various kinds. Hollis noted other buildings off to the right.

"What's over there?" she asked Ryne quietly, not wanting to disturb the other patrons enjoying their quiet evening.

"I think those are mainly barns for storage and making the wine. This smaller but nice two-story building is the NamaStays Inn. It's the main check in area. They have several small cabins you can rent, then come inside here for meals . . . like a B&B, I think. My mom and I stayed in one when we first arrived, but I didn't really partake of all its amenities. I'm sure we could ask at the bar, if you're interested."

"No." Hollis almost panicked. "I mean, no thanks, not right now anyway." She wasn't quite ready to encounter a Blackstone yet.

Thinking of that, she stretched out her hunter senses but only felt the faint hum of someone off in the distance.

Ryne frowned, but moved into the patio area anyway. "Let's sit and have some wine. Enjoy the music and ambiance here."

Hollis nodded and followed him into a large room, rustic and modern from floor to ceiling with concrete floors and horizontal wood paneling on the walls and ceiling. Fantastic yet simple light fixtures hung at various points in the room, sliced barrels hung on the walls with names of different wines, and the back of the concrete bar top area was a chalkboard filled with the season's flavors along with some town favorites.

The man behind the counter turned around. He had dark brown hair and green eyes, and he didn't give off a witch hunter's vibe. Not a Blackstone. Hollis relaxed.

CHAPTER 6

"*H*ow can I help you two?" He looked up and noticed Ryne with a smile. "Hey, Ryne! Good to see you, buddy. Who's your friend?"

"Brock, how are you, man?" He pulled Hollis next to him. "This is Hollis Black. She's in from out of town, and I thought I'd show her a few of the town's finest establishments." He winked at Brock, who seemed to be caught on Hollis's face.

Quickly Brock recovered and stuck out his hand. "Nice to meet you, Hollis. Welcome to Stone Falls Winery. Would you both like to try our newest bottle for this summer?"

Brock pulled out two clean wine glasses and placed them in front of Ryne and Hollis. At their consent, he expertly poured a small amount into each glass for them to taste. He went on to describe the flavor and what went into the production.

"Would you like to try some of our other wines?" Brock asked.

Hollis shook her head. "This one. This is the one I want," she said with a smile of satisfaction on her face. Brock nodded and poured her a full glass.

"Ryne? How about you? Want to try a deeper red?"

Ryne squished his mouth to the side. "In all honesty, I'm not much of a wine guy. You all don't have anything else available here, do ya?" he asked sheepishly.

Brock's eyes lit up, and his expression took on one of secrecy and mischief. He leaned in close and whispered, "Actually, I've been working on some micros in the basement. Wanna try what I've got cookin'?"

At Ryne's sly smile, Brock slammed his hand on the counter with excitement. "Give me a sec. I'll go grab you something."

"No worries, I'm going to the men's room." Ryne turned to Hollis. "Will you be all right here? I'll be right back. If you want to grab a table out by one of the fire barrels, I'll join you."

She smiled and lifted her wine glass. "That's where I'll be."

She ambled over to a small table and sat. With her glass of heaven, and the warmth of fire at her side, she gazed up at the mountain again and allowed herself to imagine what her life might be like if she weren't who she was but instead a normal townsperson. Perhaps she'd have a Friday night ritual where she would meet up with Callie, Michaela, and their friends for a quick glass of wine. The pretend life made her smile.

But that wasn't her life. And she wasn't a normal girl who could simply move to a new town and settle down, maybe try a real relationship with Ryne and grow old . . . older.

"Girl, you are in over your head. What in the name of all that is holy are you doing in Havenwood Falls?" a woman's voice harshly whispered as she took her seat across from Hollis, startling her back into her reality.

Hollis's eyes grew wide as saucers. "Letitia?"

She was uncertain the woman before her was the same one she had once known as a little girl. The woman had aged since the last time Hollis had seen her. Witch hunters—full hunters—aged at a slow rate if they took the lives of witches on the regular, but even if not, they still aged slower than the average human. Her father, Dante, was somewhere close to two hundred, she thought.

"Hollis Blacks—"

"Shhh, Letti. It's Black. Hollis Black." Hollis stared intently at

Letti, willing her to hear her out. Of all the Blackstones she could have run into, Letti might be the only one to lend a sympathetic ear, having spent time with Dante's rogues herself once upon a time.

The older Blackstone raised an eyebrow. "Why are you here?"

"I'm visiting a friend, Ryne Calloway. I'm not hunting."

Letitia narrowed her eyes in disbelief. "How did you even find us?" Letti asked with growing concern. "Is your father on his way?"

"Like I said, I'm here with Ryne." Hollis expertly evaded the truth with a truth of her own. "And no, he isn't on his way."

Letitia frowned. "Hollis. If your dad finds us, all we know and love here will be destroyed. Do you not see that?"

Hollis paused and looked around. "Maybe. But if he could only see what I'm beginning to, maybe he could grow to love it, too." She said the last as an unconvinced question.

"I thought that once, too. But I'm sorry, he won't change." She paused and leaned into Hollis. "Does the Court know you're here?"

"I knew there had to be some kind of leadership council. No. And I don't want them to. Can't we keep this between just us, Aunt Letti?"

Letitia scowled. "I'm sorry, dear, but I will have to inform them, especially as a former member. Your presence here brings danger to us all. You need to talk to the Blackstones and announce your arrival to Lilith. She's on the Court."

"Please, Letti, I just need a little time. I'm . . . I'm having fu—"

"Hi, Ms. Blackstone," Ryne said pleasantly as he approached the table. "I see you met Hollis."

Letti hesitated, then a small smile grew on her face. "I did indeed. I couldn't have one of our fine customers sitting all alone."

Hollis visibly relaxed and offered Letti the briefest smile.

"How did you two meet?"

"Fate," Ryne jumped in before Hollis could say anything. He winked at Letti, and she laughed.

"I'd say so. Well, I'll let you kids enjoy your evening." She got up from the table and reached for Hollis's hand. "Don't be a stranger, dear. You really should meet the rest of my family and the owners of this vineyard while you're here."

Hollis heard the message loud and clear. Tell the Blackstones she was in town or she would do it for her. Letti wouldn't have a choice.

"I would like that, thank you."

Just then, Brock brought out a pilsner glass filled with a dark microbrew with a thick froth of purple-tinted foam at the top.

"Oh man, you delivered!" Ryne rubbed his hands together. "What do you have for me?"

"You'll have to tell me what you think. It's a porter. I presented it last month at the plate-painting event, so it's been dubbed the Purple Pig Porter."

Ryne took the glass and sipped off the top.

"I see you've met my nephew, Brock Blackstone, already." Letti bored the words into Hollis's eyes. Then she turned to Brock. "I was just telling this young woman she would need to meet the rest of our family soon."

Brock looked at her again. "You look so familiar. Are you sure you haven't been here before?"

"Positive. I've been told I have a familiar face." Hollis gave a shaky smile.

"Excellent beer, man! This I can definitely enjoy. Thanks," Ryne said, taking his seat. Brock put his arm around Letti and escorted her away.

"Have a nice evening," she called over her shoulder. "Remember what I told you, dear."

Hollis's hand shook with a slight tremor. She hoped Ryne couldn't see it. She sipped on her wine to calm her nerves. Her timeline just got bumped up even further.

CHAPTER 7

*A*fter, Ryne walked her back to Whisper Falls Inn and said good night. They made a plan to meet up late the next morning for a hike to see the famous falls for which the town was named. But Hollis couldn't shake the feeling that if she didn't do something right away, her time in Havenwood Falls would come to an abrupt end.

And she wasn't ready for her time to end—for more reasons now than only her mission.

Before she and Ryne had left the vineyard, she ducked her head into the main office at NamaStays to ask Letitia for directions, which she followed as she walked up to Blackstone Road and then west to Havenwood Heights—the old money part of town, if the mansions and large iron gate had anything to say about it. Letti had given her the address to the Blackstones' house.

Hollis found herself standing in front of the Blackstone family home, tingles climbing up her neck at the presence of hunters, with her hand outstretched to ring the doorbell. It proved unnecessary as the door flung open with four Blackstone faces staring back at her, their mouths about to land on the floor.

"It was you!" Macy gasped. "In Callie's earlier, I sensed you."

Hollis nodded. "You did. I wasn't ready to meet you. I was afraid you would jump to conclusions and not give me the chance to explain myself."

"Come in off the street. We don't need the gossiping neighbors finding more to talk about." The petite woman with a fierce blond bob and blue eyes had to be Lilith, according to Hollis's limited knowledge. They moved aside and allowed her to enter. She could tell each of them had their guard up. Hollis couldn't get a read on the older man, so she assumed he was human like Brock, but the younger boy—the same boy she saw earlier at Napoli's—she got a different energy reading from. His hunter essence repeatedly fluctuated and dampened.

"Welcome to our home. I'm Reggie, this is my wife Lilith, our daughter Macy, and our youngest son Brice." Reggie's words were kind enough, but she could hear the strength in his tone. This was his home, and he would do what was necessary to protect his family, even if he was not powerful enough to take out a hunter.

"I'm Hollis Black. I met Letitia and Brock earlier tonight, and they suggested I come introduce myself to you."

"Why are you here?" Lilith asked, straight to the point, her stature tall and unmoved.

"I'm on vacation. I have been spending time with a friend, Ryne Calloway. I mean no harm while I am here. I wanted to respect your territory, though, and let you know I am temporarily in town."

Macy didn't say much, but she watched Hollis intently, making her uncomfortable. But what the little girl didn't know was Hollis had been around the block for longer than Macy had, and she could hold her own. Lilith, on the other hand, would be a fight if it came down to it, but she seemed distracted.

"Hey, I saw you with Ryne at Napoli's tonight," Brice mentioned.

"I saw you as well. You like to skateboard?" she asked, trying to make nice. He nodded and flicked the hair out of his eyes that continued to find its way back.

"Well, Hollis, we appreciate you announcing your arrival to us. You will have to officially check in with the Court of the Sun and the Moon and let them know you're here. You have twenty-four hours from when you first arrived. Addie will register you as a temporary visitor. They like to keep track of all supernaturals who come into and out of Havenwood Falls."

"Mom, don't you think you should do that—inform the Court, I mean," Macy protested. Her frown indicated she wasn't happy with her mother at the moment. Lilith glared at Macy with a quick flash of her eyes—a look that said *don't question me in front of strangers*.

"You know I will, dear—I have an obligation after all—but I wanted to give Hollis here the chance to prove herself," Lilith countered.

"You'll have to forgive us, Hollis. We were in the middle of a family . . . conversation when you showed up," Reggie explained. Just then the front door opened and shut, and Brock entered the great room.

"Are you a member of the group of witch hunters associated with Dante Blackstone?" Lilith asked straight out.

"I used to be, but left them some time ago in hopes of a newer way. Their methods are so archaic and harsh. I wanted to see if there was more for me out in the world. A more peaceful coexistence, you know?" Hollis explained, her words full of lies, and yet . . . there might have actually been more truth to them than she had ever realized.

Lilith's gaze caught Macy's with a question. Hollis only caught the look because she happened to notice at the right moment. Macy spoke blatantly. "No, I don't recognize her from my time there. But . . . several hunters were away on missions, too."

"Hey, guys, you'll never guess who I met at the vineyard today . . ." Brock stopped in his tracks, and his eyes lingered on Hollis before quickly surveying each of his family members. "Hollis Black—who is now in our living room." He seemed deflated his news was no longer pertinent. "I didn't realize she was a hunter, of course. Aunt Letti informed me of a strange hunter in town, and I put it together." He sheepishly looked over to Hollis. "Sorry, I didn't mean you were strange . . . more a stranger though." He sighed. "I'm going to shut up now."

Macy snorted, and Brice elbowed Brock playfully and whispered, "Smooth, bro."

"It's all right. I am a stranger, and perhaps a bit strange too." She attempted to laugh it off, but even to her own ears it sounded hollow and wrong. She'd never had trouble playing a part before, but she unexpectedly had trouble playing this part with these people. Something in Hollis wanted to burst out with the truth and be done with it.

"I won't keep you. It's already late. I just wanted to come by before too much time went by. I didn't want any misunderstandings." Hollis turned to go.

"How long will you be staying?" Macy asked before she got to the door.

"Not much longer. Probably through the bonfire—I've heard a lot about that. It sounds magical." Hollis winked and walked out the front door. After she shut the door, she could hear Macy loud and clear.

"I don't trust her, or believe her for that matter."

"Remember, Macy, where would we be now if someone hadn't given your ancestor, Marie Blackstone, the benefit of the doubt and taken the risk of friendship? We need to give her a chance first," Reggie said.

"What if someone gets hurt because of it?" Brice maturely asked.

"Is that our risk to take?" Macy added in agreement.

Hollis didn't want to hear anymore. They were hesitant, as they should be, but they were going to give her a short leash with a limited amount of time. Now she had to be on her guard and walk on eggshells even more. For all intents and purposes, they appeared to be a regular family with regular faults and shortcomings, but they also cared for one another and their town. Even in her brief encounter, she could see the siblings love and the parents' protectiveness. She still needed to figure out how they participated in the town. Were they the pawns her father believed they were, under the control and brainwashing of the witches? She needed to find out the truth now more than ever.

CHAPTER 8

The next day, Hollis met Ryne at the gazebo in the town square. He leaned against one of its sides, waiting for her with a big smile on his face. It was another lovely day in Havenwood Falls, and it being Friday, the townsfolk seemed to be out in full force, even more than the day before.

"What's going on? Are there always this many people hanging out?" Hollis asked, watching people coming and going with bags and boxes filled with plants, vegetables, and crafts.

"In the summer, we have a farmers' market in Cook's Corner Park. It's tomorrow, so they're setting up for it. It's just west of the square about six blocks, by the cemetery and the schools. Do you want to see?"

Hollis thought about it. The cemetery sounded intriguing. Another day. "No. I want to stick with the plan. See the falls." She stuck out one of her feet. "See? Even wore my new hiking boots."

Ryne tried not to laugh. "Okay, but we'll take it easy since they aren't broken in yet."

"Why?" She scrunched up her face.

"You'll get the mother of all blisters if you hike all day in shoes not previously broken in."

She could actually feel her face start to heat. Was she blushing? "I didn't think of that."

"No worries. We'll take a leisurely stroll to the falls and not go too far up. It will still be a sight to see from any angle."

She smiled, pleased he wasn't upset his plans were changed. Hollis relaxed and found she actually looked forward to spending the time with Ryne.

"We'll take my car since it's still a bit of a walk to the trailhead. That'll save your feet a bit. I'm parked right over there." He pointed to a spot along the side of the road in front of Madame Tahini's and, of course, Coffee Haven. Noting where her gaze went, he added, "I thought we could grab a coffee to go, too."

Hollis smiled. The boy knew all the right moves. "Definitely."

They leisurely walked in that direction, but Ryne suddenly stiffened. Hollis noted the change and under the guise of shielding her eyes from the sun, she followed his gaze across the street. He stared at a man who looked to be in his late twenties, tall and lean, wearing a flannel shirt, jeans, and work boots. And though he had on a hat and sunglasses, from the way he paused and turned toward them, Hollis had no doubt the guy stared right back at Ryne.

"He a friend of yours?" Hollis nodded toward the man.

Ryne snapped out of it and rubbed his eyes, but Hollis caught a quick glimpse of red rings around his irises. Whoa.

He huffed out a harsh laugh. "Uh. No, not with Orlon Laroc."

"Do you have a problem with him?" Something in Hollis rose up in defense of Ryne. She would introduce that Laroc fellow to her double-edged blade if Ryne wanted her to.

"Don't worry about him. Come on, let's get our coffee."

After quickly grabbing the coffee, they took Ryne's beat-up Ford pickup and drove straight up Eleventh and took a left on Blackstone Road, following it past Havenwood Heights to Alverson Road.

"Where we get out is just up here!" Ryne looked at her with excitement. "You're going to love this, Hollis."

Hollis watched him with a fascination unlike any other she had felt before. "I don't get you. You're excited about so many things. Is it real? Are you truly that happy with life?"

Ryne paused and looked at her, really looked at her. "I am. I've had reasons not to be, but in the end, I'm grateful for life."

"Why?" she prodded with genuine curiosity.

Ryne seemed to think about it, then made a decision, nodding to himself. "The place I grew up was very harsh and demanding. It wasn't easy for us where we used to live, especially for my mom. It crushed my spirit. And after my father died, my mom and I took our chance—the opportunity—and left, looking for a new life. A safer, more personable life."

"It sounds like you lived in a community or something, maybe not so unlike this one?" Hollis ventured a guess.

He laughed again. "Way different than this one. Here the people care about this town and each other. Everyone is allowed to be themselves as long as they don't hurt anyone else. My mom and I are free to be ourselves here." A sadness crept into Ryne's eyes at the mention of his mom.

Hollis listened and took in everything he said and didn't say, trying to read between the lines. She so wished she could figure out what his other half was; then maybe what he said would make more sense. The more curious thing? She actually was interested in finding out more about him. Her heart smiled a little.

She hadn't even realized how much they had walked until Ryne stopped.

With arms outstretched, Ryne revealed the most breathtaking sight Hollis had ever seen before her. "There she is. The falls."

Directly in front of her was a large glistening pool of the most refreshing-looking water. Casting her gaze up along the edges of the shore, she saw the source of the sound. Water cascaded from several stories above them at an intense rate, creating a power and energy all its own.

"Wow." Hollis couldn't bring herself to say anything else. The sight was awe-inspiring. She understood why her ancestors, and anyone from Havenwood Falls, would be drawn there. She crouched down onto her knees and bent over to peer into the crystalline pool. Reflected back at her was her image, warbled and wavy. The water smoothed to a flat glass, reflecting her face as she always saw herself in the mirror. As she looked again, the water warbled and smoothed again then showed her another version of herself—not too different from how she looked now, only softer and filled with joy and peace. Her heart ached with longing to know that person, what she was like, and how she was different than who she knew now. Hollis dipped her hand into the cool water and swirled her fingers through the reflection.

"I wouldn't touch—" Ryne started to say, but he was too late.

"The water?" Hollis looked up at him with curious eyes, but ended up having to squint with the sun in her eyes. Ryne, however, seemed to be staring at her with just as curious, if not skeptical, eyes in return. "What's wrong?" she asked, standing again.

"Nothing." He took a step back then inhaled slowly, absorbing the air around him. "It's so peaceful here. It's really a sanctuary for all kinds, you know?"

Hollis found his response strange and wondered if she had done something.

"Hey, can we hike around a bit? You know, before my feet blister." She smiled and held out one of her feet.

He smiled, shook off whatever strangeness had just happened, and reached for her hand.

"Absolutely."

They hiked around for the better part of the day then decided to call it quits. Hollis took her shoes off and rubbed her feet.

"Hey, do you want to go to the Moons in the Mist Bonfire with me tomorrow?" Ryne asked.

Hollis hesitated.

"Unless you already have someone to go with, then it's not a big deal. I just thought with the whole not knowing anyone thing you might be available." Ryne shrugged as if it were no biggie.

Hollis playfully slugged him in the upper arm. She caught

herself and actually looked at her fist. She had never done anything playful like that before.

"Yes. I'll go with you."

Ryne smiled and grabbed her hand unexpectedly. It was nothing more than a simple hand hold, but it warmed Hollis deep within her chest. She couldn't stop staring at her hand in his.

Ryne started to pull away. "Sorry, I should've asked first. I know you're not one for affection."

"I . . . I like it." Choosing not to think, but only to feel, she squeezed his hand and laced her fingers between his. When her gaze found his eyes, the depth of joy and sincerity of heart she saw in his face almost floored her. How could anyone like him be a bad thing? He obviously wasn't doing bad things with his magic, if he even knew he had it at all.

Maybe not all witches needed to be extinguished.

Maybe her father was wrong on that front. What if he was wrong on all fronts? Her chest tightened, and her heart rate sped up. Hollis could barely breathe. What was happening to her? She'd feel it if Ryne had put some kind of spell on her—at least one of a magical sort.

"I'll drop you off at the inn," Ryne started to say. His words snapped Hollis out of the life-altering state she'd been in.

"Oh, wait. I'm not staying there anymore." She quickly remembered she had checked out that morning.

"You're not? Everything okay?"

"Sure. I just felt it was time to move on." She looked out the window as they approached the Stone Falls Winery. "Actually, you can drop me off at the vineyard. I'm renting one of the cabins. I thought it might be nice to see different parts of the town." She shrugged. Plus, she subscribed to the adage "Keep your friends close and your enemies closer." She'd also been avoiding a run-in with Addie Beaumont, despite Michaela Petran's efforts to see her registered as a visitor.

"Well, I guess we're here then." Ryne pulled into the small gravel parking lot in front of the building with a sign indicating NamaStays Inn.

"Yep, this is me." Hollis didn't move except to pick her boots up off the ground. She hesitated and turned back to Ryne, who looked like he was searching for something else to say. "Thank you for showing me the falls. I had a good time." Hollis frowned, unsure if that was what she should say. Truthfully, she had never been on a real date before. She had always been too busy and focused on killing witches. She'd never tried to date one. If her father could see her now.

"I'd like to see you again, Hollis. I feel this deep pull in"—he thumped his hand on his chest—"in here when I'm with you. I don't really know what it means, but I want to see where this could go. I know it's fast, and I don't really know anything about you than the little glimpses you let me see, but—"

Hollis cut him off, planting her lips onto his. He moaned and tried to return her kiss, but her position in the truck was less than ideal and a little awkward. She quickly pulled back, and as embarrassment flooded her cheeks, she clutched the handle to open her door. Ryne grabbed her elbow and gently turned her back to him. He slowly moved toward her face, guiding her chin close to him with his outside hand while his other hand reached behind her head. His mouth found hers and gently started moving over her lips. Hollis couldn't help the groan of pleasure erupting from her chest like a damn cat. He teased her lips, and she found herself wanting more from him. Emboldened by his kiss, Hollis readjusted her position and climbed onto his lap. The intensity of their kiss grew, and the oxygen in the car diminished. Hollis's chest grew unexpectedly hot . . . too hot. She leaned back to find Ryne's eyes not only rimmed again with red, but also his normal gray electrified.

"Wow . . ." She leaned in to say something about his eyes, then caught herself. She breathed deep. "I mean, I've done that before, but . . . with you . . . I don't know, it was different." Hollis was at a loss for words as she caught her breath. Her stomach erupted with damn butterflies. She felt giddy like a teenager, which she was most definitely not. Why had kissing Ryne felt different? A little voice whispered to her in the back of her mind, *"Because you have feelings for him—half witch and all."*

Ryne's gaze roamed from the top of her head, over her face, and further south, studying everything about her. No man had ever looked at her before like that. When she peered deep into his eyes, now back to their normal soft gray, she could still see magic, but only what was naturally him. Or perhaps his witch side and his man side were not exclusive. Perhaps all of it was what made him who he was. And she liked who he was.

Ryne tenderly swiped a piece of hair out of her face, sliding his fingers across her forehead. A sudden vibration in her back pocket arrested Hollis out of her little bubble of happiness—happiness! She wondered if that was what happiness felt like. She pulled out her cell phone, surprised to find all of a sudden it had service, when previously it had been pretty spotty since she'd arrived. Reading the screen, her heart plummeted to her feet.

Her screen read: Dante Blackstone. Her father. The infamous witch hunter who had sent her to Havenwood Falls on a mission. And here she was not only with a witch but KISSING one.

Scrambling off Ryne and back to her seat, Hollis grabbed her boots. "I . . . I have to go. I'm sorry, Ryne."

"Is everything okay? Was that too fast?" His expression looked worried as she hurried out of the door.

"Yes, no, I mean, I'm sorry. I have to go." She held up her phone. "It's my dad, and if I don't answer, he'll worry."

Understanding dawned on his face. "Gotcha. Go take your call. Maybe later?"

She nodded and waved, then ran around the inn entrance, following the path to her private little cabin in the back of the vineyard.

CHAPTER 9

"Hello? . . . Dad? Can you hear me? The reception isn't good here." Hollis answered her phone after the third time in a row her father had called. She could practically hear the irritation ringing through her phone.

"Where am I? I'm here. I made it." She paused, and a weak smile emerged on her face based on some praise her father had said, even though he mentioned he didn't catch all her words. "I found the other Blackstones and am learning about the dynamics of the town with the witches," she explained. He said more, and she was quiet as she walked into her little cabin. But frustrated she kept losing the call again, she stepped back outside.

"Sorry Dad, I can't hear you well. Yes, the source was right. It's in Colorado in the mountains somewhere . . . What? Hello? Are you there? Oh, there you are. I don't know where exactly. I came on a bus in the dark." Hollis gazed up at the mountain and then out at the beautiful rows of vines filled with plump grapes ready to be harvested. She wondered what it would feel like to mash grapes within her hands and to work the land. Getting distracted, she almost dropped the phone when her dad yelled into the receiver.

"Yes, I'm here. Bad service, I told you," she lied. The last time she had lied to her father, she was little and had to stay in a dark room alone for an entire day, though it felt like several. She never did it again.

"Yes, I'm staying focused. What are you looking for with the witches? Plans? Organization? Magic? I don't know what I'm looking for." Listening, she kicked a rock from her path and felt her chest cavity close in on itself as her father listed the many things he wanted to know about, such as the hierarchy, who the leaders were, where their sacred circles were, what kind of weapons they had, what the procedure was if they were invaded, etc.

"I'll check back in a couple days with more information. Okay. Bye, Dad." She hung up. "Yeah, love you too," she muttered sarcastically under her breath.

"Not the affectionate one, is he?" Letti asked from the edge of the vineyard, far enough away to not be detected by her hunter vibes but not quite far enough to not overhear her conversation.

"No, never has been," Hollis answered her question with a previously unrealized hint of regret.

"Neither was mine. I turned out okay." Letti consoled her with a wink.

Hollis smiled. Still unnerved, she asked, "How long have you been there?"

"Oh, not long." Letti waved her concern off. "I just came to see how you were faring."

Hollis crossed her arms over her chest. "You mean you were checking up on me."

Letti smiled but didn't correct her. "Have you had a chance to chat with the Blackstones yet?"

"I did, actually. They were quite . . . welcoming."

Letti laughed. "In their own way, I'm sure."

Hollis also laughed. "They don't know who I am yet, Letti. I need a little more time."

Letti frowned and bit her lower lip. "I can't be an accomplice to this, Hollis."

"No one will know you knew. I'll keep your part a secret."

"Only because I'm hoping you can see what I see in this town."

"I'm afraid your wish may bring me consequences." She sighed. "The Blackstones want me to check in with the Court. Where do I find them?"

"Oh I'm sure they will find you. Addie Beaumont has been on the search already. She's a powerful witch and will want to register you as a visitor."

Well, Hollis couldn't take the chance of Addie Beaumont reading her with magic or temporarily registering her and being able to trace her or her heritage. She wasn't sure how registering worked, but she couldn't risk it. She would lie and tell the Blackstones she had an appointment to meet with Addie—and if they followed up to see if she met with her? Well, plans get changed, don't they? Hollis planned on not staying in one location long enough to be found.

"Have a nice night, dear. Looked like you were having one before your phone call." Letti pursed her lips and chuckled, then turned to leave.

"Why, you little spy," Hollis teased, slightly offended she got caught. Then she remembered that no one truly knew her. They weren't going to tell her father on her. She could be whomever she wanted to be in Havenwood Falls; the thought caused her to think.

"Good night, Hollis." Letti had told Hollis she didn't live on site, and she left every night promptly at six unless she had an evening Yoga in the Vines class, which only happened a couple nights a week. At least that's what the sign had announced.

"Right. A good night. You too," Hollis said, distracted as she went into her cabin for the evening. At the door, she stopped and looked up at the mountains with fresh perspective, inhaling deep and slow. "I could be whoever I want to be here."

Ryne had told her he had to go to work at McCabe & Sons Construction. So the next day Hollis decided to try her hand at roaming the town on her own. She had been bombarded with Ryne's presence since she first arrived in the small town. Then he started to grow on her. Hollis still couldn't understand why he wanted to hang around her. She thought of their kiss with a smile, and her body heated all over again.

A jarring thought suddenly occurred to her: he could be a spy. What if he was a part of the town Court she kept hearing about, and he had been keeping his eye on her since the beginning? The thought didn't sit well with her. He hadn't come off suspicious at all, and she'd been trained to be a good reader of people and intentions. Plus she had pretty good natural instincts as a hunter. No, she didn't think he was anything but who he portrayed himself to be. She still didn't know what his other half was, but she found herself becoming lulled by his presence and not agitated by the witch essence that normally assaulted her on a constant basis. Instead it was like her body acclimated to his presence—only his. She still felt the same agitation climbing her arms into her neck, but she had been a hunter for so long, she knew how to control the sensations and not let the feelings control her. Hollis touched her neck at the mark she'd been born with, the mark that declared her a witch hunter; it had always been a part of her. With Ryne, she decided she would trust her instincts.

Hollis casually strolled from the vineyard toward the town square, weaving through neighborhoods to see parts of town tourists wouldn't normally see. The town, the places people lived, the strangers offering her a wave and a friendly hello on the street—it was a mix she thought existed only on television, and yet she found it genuine and endearing.

I wonder what kind of home I would live in if I lived here? Hollis wondered to herself, looking at the cute craftsman homes and then observing the nice well-kept apartment building as she headed into the square. She would never allow herself to even ponder such a question on a mission, but since she was playing the part of Hollis Black visiting a friend, and no one knew the difference, she figured she'd embrace it and see what it felt like to dream.

She passed Broastful Brew but sensed a heavy witch presence

and decided to keep going back to her new favorite, Coffee Haven. Plus, she couldn't forget the taste of those blueberry scones!

When she entered the café, the smell of roasted coffee beans and baking deliciousness hit her all at once. Her traitorous body wanted to close her eyes and swim in the magic of her olfactory senses; instead, she willed herself to stay present. Hollis sensed a couple of witches, but decided she couldn't avoid them all. Waiting in line, she took the time to observe the shop and the people in it. But as soon as she did, she regretted it.

At a table amongst the crowd sat Callie, the owner of Callie's Consignments, and two other women. One woman—the one with light brown hair, black-framed glasses, and tats running up and down her arms—she was pretty sure was Addie Beaumont, the witch whom she'd been avoiding. The other, a petite woman with long brown hair and green eyes, she hadn't seen before. There was a brief conversation between the three before Callie extended her hand and waved her over. Hollis hesitated. She could sense the one girl was a witch and a strong one at that. She wasn't sure what the other woman was, but she could sense dark magic surrounding her—not black witch magic, but something else entirely. If Hollis refused and left right then, she would be admitting guilt of some kind and cause a scene. So instead, she smiled and gave Callie a short wave in return.

"I'm going to order, then I'll come over," Hollis said, pointing that she was next in line. Callie gave her a curt nod and waved her to stay put, not rude but just to the point. That was why Hollis liked her. Callie showed you who she was—no games.

Not like the game Hollis now played. Regret bubbled in her chest. It shouldn't matter. She wouldn't see these people again after the mission. But what if she did? Hollis Black could even see them being friends, maybe.

"Hi, Hollis, what can I get you this morning?" Willow asked with a smile. Taken aback at first that Willow remembered her name, Hollis paused, then smiled. She realized she liked it.

58

"Morning. Just coffee, black please. And a blueberry scone, if you have any?"

Willow smiled. "Of course I do. Your coffee will be right up if you want to wait a second." Willow was suddenly pushed forward with a slight burst of shock, then she laughed and looked down behind her. A little girl with hair so blond it was almost white clung onto Willow's leg. "Hang on, sweetie. Mommy's working."

"She's yours? How old is she?" Hollis asked. The little girl looked up at her with big, surprisingly golden eyes and gave her a toothy grin. No hesitation. No judgment. Just joy. Hollis couldn't help but smile back at her and wave.

"She is. This is Arabella. She's just over one and a half. I thought she was playing in the office with Harlow."

"Sorry, Willow. I opened the door for a second, and she escaped. You're a little escape artist, aren't you?" the other woman, who must have been Harlow, said with a playful tone as she scooped up the little girl, kissed her cheek, and held her. Hollis watched with interest as the tingling sensations climbed her arms. Harlow, too, was a witch.

But Willow watched Hollis instead. "Maybe someday you'll have this too. You could, you know."

The spell was broken, and Hollis cocked her head. "Can you read minds or something?" Hollis whispered.

"Something like that," Willow cheekily responded with a wink. "Here's your coffee and scone to go, Hollis. Have a good day."

Hollis grabbed her coffee off the counter and her scone in a paper bag. She turned back to the little girl staring intently at her just as her mama had—as if she knew too much.

Walking around a couple tables filled with people, she made her way to Callie and the others. "Morning, Callie."

"Hollis, these are my friends Harper Sinclair and Addie Beaumont," she introduced.

Addie. Witch. The one Michaela had already warned about her. Confirmed. Great, now Addie knew what she looked like. There'd be no hiding after this.

"I'm Hollis Black," she said with a forced smile.

"Would you like to sit?" Addie asked, pulling out the fourth chair at their table.

"Thank you, but I'm not staying." She held up her paper bag as if that proved it.

Harper was quiet and smiled but she kept looking around Hollis as if she was seeing more than what was right in front of her. It was unnerving, to say the least. Hollis needed to get out of there.

"Will you be around much longer?" Callie asked.

"Not too much. I'm staying for the bonfire tonight, then I'm not sure."

"Going with Ryne?" Callie asked suggestively. Addie slugged her with her elbow, but Callie shrugged, unconcerned. "What? I saw them together."

"I am, yes." Hollis grew more uncomfortable.

"Is Ryne who you know here in town?" Addie questioned, her eyes tightening, as though scrutinizing her.

Hollis hesitated. Aside from the witch vibes Hollis felt up her arms, she also got the impression Addie wasn't happy with her, though she seemed nice enough on the outside.

Hollis nodded. "He's my friend."

"But maybe more than that?" Callie slyly added.

Hollis's gaze flickered around the room, unsure of who was listening. She cleared her throat. "I don't know what you mean."

Callie smirked wickedly. "I like you, Hollis."

But Harper didn't look so sure.

"I need to take off, but you ladies have a good one. Nice to meet you." Hollis couldn't leave fast enough.

"You too," Addie and Harper both said.

"Hey, I like your shoes. They're much more . . . you," Callie said with an appreciative nod at Hollis's feet. Instead of the tennis shoes she had first seen her in, Hollis wore her black buckle-up boots over gray skinny jeans. Something about Callie's approval made Hollis feel more like herself than the tourist she pretended to be. Perhaps she was someone in the middle of the two. Hollis wished she knew. Life was simpler before she arrived.

As she left the table and reached the door, she heard Harper whisper, "A lot of darkness surrounds that girl . . . a lot of death."

Goosebumps erupted down Hollis's spine. How could she know that? Is that what she was seeing—ghosts? The thought made Hollis want to run until she couldn't run anymore. Instead she casually walked away from Coffee Haven, not willing to let Harper's words or the type of people in the town rattle her. But that was exactly how she felt—rattled.

CHAPTER 10

*A*fter Hollis's encounter at the coffee shop, she needed to walk off the strangeness she was seeing more of in Havenwood Falls. At first it appeared so serene and tranquil. But she had the feeling a storm of supernaturals and their darkness and secrets percolated beneath. That thought alone comforted her to know she wasn't the worst being who might be in town. Perhaps the darkness she carried, the monster she was, could fit in a place like this.

Unaware of where she'd been heading, she was surprised to find herself in front of the town cemetery. Slowly Hollis wandered inside. She had always liked cemeteries and would often find the oldest one in the various towns and cities they ended up in. She could find peace there and take a few minutes to herself—unless she had hunted in that particular area. She was afraid one day she would be haunted by the ghosts of those witches she had removed from the world. The thought hadn't bothered her too much until now. Grateful she had never been in Havenwood Falls before, she felt safe to stay for a few minutes. Rows and rows of precisely placed headstones dotted the ground, and evenly distributed benches were accompanied by clusters of trimmed trees. For the age of

Havenwood Falls, Hollis expected older graves and wondered where those were.

As she continued to walk, the thought occurred to her that Blackstones in their final rest should reside there. Wandering around for several minutes, she discovered there oddly weren't any. Something shimmered and caught her eye. Hollis walked to where pretty crystals hung on a tree. Out of the corner of her eye another path revealed itself to her, as if beckoning her to follow. Curiosity struck her, and she continued on the path, which mysteriously led her to a stone-pillared arched tunnel that traversed under Blackstone Road.

"What's on the other side?" she whispered, not expecting a response. She looked around to ensure she was alone and bravely strode through the tunnel. To her surprise, the tunnel opened to another section—a hidden section—revealing the type of cemetery Hollis had originally been expecting. Pausing at the entrance, she reverently absorbed the scene. These plots were much older, less pristine and orderly, but also held a serenity and beauty all their own. She wondered why the separation, unless this section was reserved for supernatural families. Hollis wondered if anyone could wander into this section or if she found it because she was herself not entirely human.

This section hummed with magic—witch magic, mixed with magic she couldn't place. Witch magic essence thrummed through her veins from her fingers to her shoulder blades, crawling up her arms. The magic was powerful and old—very old. Hollis hesitated. She had never felt the harmony of such magic working together in one place. She sensed the warning and the danger, but also the protection and the symbiosis of it. This was sacred ground.

"I mean you no harm. I'm looking for my ancestors," she whispered to the magic, in case it listened. Lightly she stepped, staying on an invisible path, guided by an invisible arm drawing her in one direction. This portion of the cemetery felt alive, not only from the strength of the magic, but actually alive. When she didn't look directly at something, she saw vines grow and twist, flowers bloom and release petals over the dead, branches bend and sway out of the corner of her eye.

Hollis gingerly walked by much older graves. Bending down, without touching them, she noticed many held runes or other magical symbols.

"I wonder what those are for," she whispered out loud. Continuing her curious meandering, she came across what appeared to be possibly the oldest graves she had seen yet. They were oddly covered with metal cages. Hollis frowned and steered herself away from those. She couldn't fathom what they were for, unless . . . Nope, she didn't want to think about horror movie–style scenarios involving zombies.

She kept on in her search. One in particular she looked for: Marie Blackstone, her father's youngest sister. The one who started the separation between the Blackstones back in the 1800s. When Macy had stayed with Dante's hunters after leaving Havenwood Falls almost two years ago, she informed Dante of Marie's passing at the turn of the century.

Noting the names on headstones, she recognized some of them from names she had heard in town: Beaumont, Fairchild, Augustine —and some she hadn't heard yet: Bishop, Mills, among others.

Finally she found the name she'd been seeking: Blackstone. Several were familiar, but others must have been Blackstone hunters from Marie's line. Finally she saw Judson Carter Blackstone, and right next to him was his wife, Marie Marcella Blackstone. Hollis walked right up next to it and placed her hand on top of the headstone. She couldn't see or hear ghosts, but the stone warmed under her hand, and she felt welcomed. She hadn't expected that.

"You know who I am?" she whispered, not at all feeling strange speaking to a gravesite. "Your brother sends his love." Hollis laughed darkly as she said the words, sure Marie knew the truth of it. "I found my way here. I'm sure you know why. But I have all these conflicting emotions and thoughts. Part of me sees what you were seeking when you left my father and the others all those years ago. I see the camaraderie this town has no matter the races, no matter the secrets. I'm sure they have their conflicts like any family, but that's what it feels like—family. And I just figured that out." Hollis huffed, struck by the absurdity of her mission and essentially her whole life.

"My life is a sham. What I thought was family has been an organization intent on using whoever they can to advance the one ideal of a madman—my father. He doesn't care about me, not really. I can't believe it took me talking to a dead person to figure that out."

Rocking back on her heels, Hollis simply stayed and absorbed the love she suddenly felt emanating from Marie's headstone. She closed her eyes, and though she knew it had to simply be the magic of the place, she allowed it and even craved it. One by one she felt additional warmth coming from Judson and then each of the other Blackstones nearby. The feeling was overwhelming.

Hollis cried. She never cried, but there in a magical cemetery, surrounded by dead ancestors freely offering her love with no judgment or stipulation, she broke down, and the tears flowed.

Several minutes passed, though to Hollis it felt like a lifetime had come and gone. A gentle stroke ran up and down her arm. Startled, she looked around, searching for the source until landing on a vine reaching down to her from a nearby tree. It was suddenly in full bloom, whereas it had only buds minutes before. The vine grew downward and stroked her arm once again, as if coaxing her to rise. She stood and felt her moment was finished. It was time for her to go.

"Thank you," she quietly said, looking at each of the Blackstone graves. "I know what I need to do."

Hollis left with renewed spirit and a new mission. She stood tall, her inner badass coming out to play, but this time tempered and softened by a redefining moment. She didn't have to be who she was trained to be.

Her phone rang. Her father's ringtone blared, as if he somehow sensed her change of heart. Quickly she left the sacred space of the old cemetery, not wanting to taint it with opening a channel to her father. Once outside the cemetery, she wiped her pants off and straightened her jacket. She steeled her shoulders and stiffened her spine.

"Dad, I was just about to call you—" She paused mid-sentence. "What? You're where? On your way to Colorado? Oh, I had no idea you were coming so soon. Why didn't you tell me?" Again she listened. "I told you the reception up here is crazy."

In her chest, Hollis felt the panic start to throw her off, but she planted her feet and deeply inhaled. He wasn't there yet. And he didn't know where to go past the city of Montrose, as far as she knew. She needed more time in the town. She *wanted* more time in the town and with Ryne. Her heart sped up at the thought of Ryne and what he'd think of her when he found out the truth. She needed to tell him right away.

"I don't have all the information you need yet. I need more time. How far away are you?" She listened and nodded as if he could see her. "I'll get it for you by then. Call me when you're in a nearby town." She hung up and squeezed her phone. She'd throw it if she didn't need it.

"Think, Hollis. He's on his way, but not here yet. Your new mission hasn't changed. What are you going to do?" Hollis paced right outside the cemetery then abruptly stopped. "I need to find the Court. I could ask Callie to call Addie. Aunt Letti said they would find me. Well, now would be a good time."

Chills went up her spine, warming at her neck, and she felt eyes on her. A hunter was near. She stormed back toward the town square and figured she'd know her next step when she saw it.

CHAPTER 11

*H*ollis strode up to the intersection of Eighth and Stuart Streets, at the corner of the town square, her stride full of focused intent with renewed purpose. The little witch hunter followed her, but she wasn't about to let Macy stop her yet. Hollis had a plan, and she needed to see it through in her own way.

Hollis was ready to march straight into either Whisper Falls Inn for Michaela or over to Callie's Consignments for Callie—either could get her in touch with Addie, so she could finally register.

Lucky for Hollis, she didn't have to go that far. Gathered right in front of City Hall stood Callie, Michaela, and Addie chatting on the grass side of the street. She swerved and made a beeline for them.

"Callie! Michaela!" Hollis called and raised her hand to get their attention. Their heads all swiveled in her direction, surprise written on their faces. Michaela smiled and waved back. Callie cocked her head, and Addie lowered her sunglasses to peer over them.

"I was just looking for you—all of you, actually," Hollis admitted as she approached closer. "I have to say something. I'm not who I said I was."

"We know," Michaela confirmed, unsurprised.

"We were waiting for you to do the right thing," Callie admonished.

"You've been dodging me, but these two—and Lilith, by the way —convinced me and the Court that you'd figure out on your own that we're not the enemy, and to give you a little more time." Addie shrugged. "I guess my girls here can read people pretty well."

"Stop!" a female voice yelled from a block away. All four of them turned to find Macy Blackstone with her phone up to her ear, running straight for them. Simultaneously, a black car pulled up right along the opposite side of the street. Letitia, Brock, and Lilith Blackstone got out of the car, followed by an older woman, who most definitely carried the Blackstone trademark look of blond hair and blue eyes.

"Shit," Hollis muttered under her breath.

"Hello, Lilith, Brock, Letti, and Eva. What brings you here together on this lovely day?" Addie asked, trying to defuse the sudden tension crackling in the air.

"Macy told us to get here right away," Lilith answered.

"Hunter business, dear. Hollis, this is Eva, Lilith's mother," Letti added, regarding the other woman.

"There's Macy now," Eva noted. Macy caught up to where they were, out of breath but quickly recovering.

"Hey, Hollis!" Ryne shouted from the other direction, getting out of his truck. He ran over with a big smile on his face.

"Oh, what a shitshow," Hollis mumbled and looked to the sky in defeat. This was going to hurt him. Her heart broke at how he might be affected by this turn of events.

"Hey, everybody!" Ryne took everyone in, along with their expressions, as he approached Hollis's side. "What's going on?" he added with suspicion.

"How is he involved?" Eva asked, confusion etched on her slightly wrinkled face. "He shouldn't be here."

"He's my friend," Hollis defended him, to her own surprise. "None of you should be here. I came to talk to Addie on my own."

"She's not who she says she is," Macy blurted out.

"She's a hunter, dear. They already know that," Letitia confirmed for the benefit of the others present.

Addie and Michaela didn't look surprised.

"Lilith already told us," Addie supplied for Macy's benefit. However, the expression on Ryne's face told her he had suspected nothing of the sort.

"*What?*" he expelled with a rush of air. Hollis couldn't bear to see his face. She refused to look at him until she had said her bit.

"No, there's more," Macy added. "I kept thinking there was something more familiar to her. But I saw her leaving the sacred part of the cemetery after spending time at the family plots. I can't believe I didn't see it sooner. And her phony name. It was so close, how did we not suspect it?" Macy deeply inhaled to replenish the air she had used rushing out the last bit of information. Then she blurted, "She's a Blackstone."

Gasps of surprise were uttered from within the group.

"We're too exposed here," Addie said quietly, looking around at those on the streets surrounding them. The afternoon sunlight was high and bright in the sky, and townspeople went about their business none the wiser. They needed to keep it that way and not cause a scene. "We need to get to the bottom of this, but not here."

"We can take her inside and call the rest of the Court," Lilith directed.

"Are you on the council? I was trying to find them," Hollis said, directing her question to Michaela.

"You don't get to speak. Not yet," Macy spat. Anger shone in her eyes as she pointed her finger at Hollis's chest. "You lied. You deceived us about who you were and why you were here."

"Why are you here?" came a low and quiet man's voice. Ryne. He had been quiet up until then. The softness of his voice, the undercurrent of pain she could hear, broke her heart. She may have lost him before she even had him.

"Addie's right. We can't do this out here. Inside, everyone," Letti said, and ushered them toward the back of the City Hall building.

"I was coming to tell you the truth, to come clean about everything," Hollis admitted as they walked across the street and to the side of the building. She crossed her arms, frustrated but not surprised it would go down in chaos and consequences.

"This should be rich, coming from you," Macy vehemently said.

Hollis snapped her head toward her with a glare that would intimidate most men. "What is your problem? You haven't even heard what I have to say."

"You're related to Dante, and a part of the rogues. That's all I need to know." Macy crossed her arms but didn't take her eyes off Hollis.

"No, it's not. You're all in danger, and I might be the only one who can help," Hollis countered.

"Not here," Addie said through clenched teeth. "We've had enough trouble lately. We don't need any of the town in a frenzy over something we don't even know about yet." She moved ahead of the group and led them around the back of City Hall to a secret door. She uttered a spell and opened the door. Hollis could feel the magic hum over her skin and glanced at the other hunters in the group. She noted the slight strain at the corners of their eyes as they, too, felt the magic flow, but there was hardly even a flinch among them. She wondered how they had perfected their control over the years, being around so many witches.

"I'm not sure I need to be here for this," Brock mentioned casually to his mom. She patted his arm.

"It's up to you. We can fill you in if you need to man Soothing Sips. Depending on what transpires here, we might need the basement ready to access," she whispered in return. Brock nodded and turned to leave. Before he passed Hollis, he stopped and looked her in the eye.

"I'm not a hunter, but I do know how to protect my family and my town. I hope I don't have to against you. You could be a great addition to our family." Then he left.

Hollis cocked her head in confusion. It sounded as if he hoped she stayed and didn't hold who she was against her. Even after she lied. Too bad Macy wasn't going to be so easy to convince, but then again, she had spent time with her father, so Hollis almost didn't blame the girl.

"You can go, too, if you want, Callie," Michaela offered.

Callie crossed her arms over her chest. "No way. I'm not missing out. Plus, aren't I an eyewitness or something?"

Michaela rolled her eyes but nodded. Hollis didn't even mind they might be talking about a hearing for her. She liked their connection and mutual respect for each other and their town. She envied that.

They entered the building and immediately descended a flight of stairs into the basement under City Hall. After a long hallway, they entered into a large room. Addie flicked her fingers, and candles erupted with flames of light within large glass globes hanging from the ceiling. Addie threw a notebook and her bag onto the desk at the back of the room. Hollis absently noted the murals of what must be a timeline of Havenwood Falls history painted on the walls. An aisle up the middle of the room with rows of chairs on either side led up to a raised dais with a space for each member of the elusive Court of the Sun and the Moon. Hollis was about to find out who made up the council.

"I texted the members, Lilith," Addie announced.

Lilith nodded, "Very good. They will be here shortly, then." She turned to Hollis. "Please have a seat at the front table facing the Court's seats."

Hollis confidently strode to the front and took the seat Lilith indicated. Lilith and Michaela continued on up to seats on the dais. Hollis was surprised to see Michaela—someone so young and so cool—was a member of the Court. Perhaps she would be willing to listen. The others sat in chairs randomly behind her. She looked to Ryne, but he sat and kept his head down. Just as she was about to turn back to the front, he lifted his head and glared directly at her. She swore she saw an orange spark erupt in his eyes, then ring his irises once more with red. It seemed to happen whenever he experienced intense emotion. She didn't think a witch could do that and wondered not for the first time what his other half was. Then he turned his head away.

She deserved that. And more. She could argue he kept his own secret from her, but this was about more than hurt feelings. She had to own what she did.

CHAPTER 12

*M*embers of the Court Hollis kept hearing about began to file into the room and make their way onto the raised dais right in front of where she sat. No one spoke to her. They barely even spoke to each other. Other than Lilith Blackstone and Michaela from the inn, she didn't know any of the other members. Addie must have been more of a secretary, since she sat and pulled out notes from the desk they passed at the back.

"Explain for the Court why have we been summoned here, Michaela." A woman with silvery-white hair in a French twist and wearing a navy blue business suit sat herself in the center, her eyes shifting from Michaela to Hollis and back again. She exuded a lot of power. Hollis had to keep herself from shivering from the effects of the woman's magic.

"Saundra, this is Hollis Blackstone," Michaela introduced. "She has been in town for two and a half days under the name Hollis Black. Lilith asked us all to give the witch hunter a chance to do the right thing and come to us. It took her a little bit, but she did."

"Yes. The coven has been on edge since she arrived." The witch named Saundra gave Hollis a pointed stare. Hollis could feel the magic seep from her pores. The witch's power was so immense, she must have been high up, if not the head of her coven. "So you did the right thing. That's good to know. But why the summons, Michaela?" She turned her sharp gaze back to her fellow Court member.

"Well," Michaela continued, "she had just come clean to Addie, Callie, and myself when Macy and the Blackstones arrived on the scene to out her as a Blackstone—one of the *rogue* Blackstones. We do not know her intentions for being in town, but—"

"I could—" Hollis began, but was quickly cut off by Saundra, who seemed to be the one in charge, glaring at her with a lifted brow.

"Hollis, you will get your chance," Michaela said before turning back to Saundra. "I was about to give her credit for coming to us. She was trying to tell us of a danger coming. She stayed at the inn and is now at NamaStays. We have observed her, as we all discussed with Lilith, and Ryne Calloway has spent time with her as well. I've not personally witnessed any ill will toward the town thus far." Michaela tilted her head, indicating she was finished, and all eyes swiveled to Saundra.

"First off, Hollis, I am Saundra Beaumont, and this is the Court of the Sun and the Moon. You are not officially on trial, but are on very thin ice. This is an opportunity for you to speak your side, and we will decide from that point. This is our town, and we protect it against all threats. Our job is to determine if you are, or bring to us, a threat."

Hollis nodded. "I understand."

She gave away nothing in her demeanor. Sitting tall and confident, she studied the Court and chose her words. She knew she hadn't done anything wrong, not really. Lied maybe, but she hadn't hurt anyone and truthfully had tried to keep to herself. This was her making a change.

"Hollis, please tell us why you are here and what danger you spoke of to Michaela, Callie, and my granddaughter, Addie," Saundra directed.

Granddaughter. Right, that would explain the witch power Addie exuded.

Hollis started from the beginning, sharing how she came to find Havenwood Falls up to her experience in the cemetery and her phone call with Dante. She even included her brief encounter at Callie's with a witch practitioner of black magic. She figured this was the place to inform them, then they could deal with it or not. It wasn't her job.

"So he's coming. I haven't told him where I am yet. Reception has been, thankfully, bad. But he knew up until the small town of Montrose. I have no doubts he'll find a way to seek out Havenwood Falls. He says you put a spell on him to keep him from it, but he has ways around things eventually." Hollis lowered her eyes momentarily. "But I've come to love your town and the potential to find out who I am outside of being a witch hunter. I've never really felt like I belonged anywhere, but this feels like it could be somewhere. I'm sorry. I didn't know he would come. This was supposed to only be an information-gathering mission."

"Unless he never planned that all along, dear, and was just using you to get here," Letitia spoke up from her seat in the audience, though no one seemed to mind.

Hollis opened her mouth to say something, to rebut her suggestion, but deep down, she knew the truth. Her father had set her up, and she didn't know to what extent.

"She used to be on the Court before Lilith," someone whispered from behind her. Hollis nodded, not caring who it was.

"He's going to call when he gets to Montrose. I'll be there to meet him when he does," Hollis said as quickly as she had decided it. Leaving Havenwood Falls was the right thing for her to do. No one would get hurt that way. She glanced with a heavy heart at Ryne out the corner of her eye. At least, no one else would get hurt.

"You're offering to leave?" Michaela asked from the platform.

Hollis looked up at her with confusion. "Isn't that what you would have me do? If I'm gone, then he won't be able to find you."

"What will he do to you, Hollis?" Lilith asked, her voice oddly low. Hollis had heard her name mentioned by her father. Apparently they had made contact years ago and again more recently, when he followed Macy back as far as he could. She wondered how much Lilith knew of her father and his ways. Judging by the pale complexion and the brief flash of fear she saw in the woman's eyes, Lilith knew more than she let on.

Hollis shrugged and turned her head. "I'll be fine. I'm his daughter." Her voice was weak, and she wouldn't have believed herself either. "I deserve whatever I get. I'm not blameless in the lifestyle he's lived. After all, I've been a lead witch hunter for several years. I'm good at my job." Hollis felt her blood run cold, and her eyes go flat. She had to convince the Court she was indeed dangerous and they needed her to go.

"If you change your mind, there are alternatives we could explore," another older woman suggested. She, too, exuded strong witch powers, but she carried herself more like the grandmotherly type. But Hollis bet she was much more than that.

"Mathilde, the girl has already made her decision. Let her go and see what comes of it," a distinguished-looking man said as he gazed at his fingernails, as if bored with the entire event. The witch magic coming from him was not only powerful and old, but almost convoluted—not quite black but definitely dangerous. She wondered why the Court kept him around.

"Roman, I was merely pointing out she didn't have to leave. But yes, I understand she made her decision."

"She will have to see it through as far as her heart will allow her," a different man said. This one was older, wiser, and ornery-looking. He simply stared at her as if reading her beginning to end like an open book. His vibe unnerved Hollis when not much did.

"Elsmed, what does that even mean?" Lilith asked, practically rolling her eyes with the tone she used.

The one she addressed as Elsmed turned and shrugged. "She will have to decide."

Hollis pinched the bridge of her nose. The Court talked in circles, and it gave her a headache. She just wanted to leave already. She didn't even know why she still sat there. Hollis stood and gave a last look at the Court, especially Michaela and Lilith, and nodded.

She turned and strode out of the room back the way she came. She heard shouting suddenly erupt behind her, and the voice initiating it pinched her heart.

"Are you just going to let her leave? Her father is dangerous," Ryne shouted.

"Are you?" Callie questioned. Hollis smiled. They weren't even friends, and yet she wished they were.

As soon as she reached the street, she found she couldn't breathe and had to run. She ran all the way back to Stone Falls Winery and NamaStays Inn. Except once she was almost there, she veered left on Blackstone Road and kept running until she reached the falls.

CHAPTER 13

*H*ollis ran up to the lake where Ryne had taken her. The water was as sparkling and clear as it was then. She watched the falls flow down from the highest point she could see. Closing her eyes, she felt the rush of power freely offered and felt the spray of the water as it kissed her face. Tingles ran up her arm as she felt another hunter approach.

She turned as Macy Blackstone emerged up the path. "You're fast," she huffed as she caught her breath.

"You could be, too, if you let yourself embrace all your gifts— you know, except the killing of witches part." Hollis shrugged, critically eyeing Macy.

Macy frowned. "After I spent time with your dad and the others, I was afraid but also determined to not let my hunter side control me. But I'm always on guard and always extra careful because my boyfriend—fiancé now"—Macy blushed, obviously not yet used to saying it out loud—"is a witch, so I don't let myself fully embrace that side of me. I don't know how."

"I could help you . . . Well, if I were staying, that is," Hollis quietly said. "You wouldn't trust me anyway, though."

Macy bit her lip in consternation. "I don't. It's true."

"Why are you here? Making sure I leave?" Hollis turned her back to Macy and bent down to the cool pool of water, cupping some in her palm.

"I wouldn't—"

Hollis brought the water to her mouth and drank it all. She raised an eyebrow to Macy. "You wouldn't what?"

"Well, at least I know the falls are okay with you." Macy frowned at the traitorous waters.

"What?"

"The water . . . Well, the magic in the water. Supposedly it'll harm those who intend to threaten our town." She shrugged, as if that was something in everyday conversation.

"The water?" Hollis whispered and cocked her head in thought, remembering Ryne having the same reaction. "The water is the source of power for the town." She looked at Macy. "And for you all? Somehow it empowers or binds you to the town, is that it?"

"Something like that." Macy suddenly looked uncomfortable, as if she had accidentally told a traitor the biggest secret the town had. Perhaps she did.

"I want you to trust me. I won't let Dante know about Havenwood Falls." Hollis stared deep into Macy's eyes, pleading with her to believe her.

"I'm here because Aunt Letti reminded me everyone deserves a second chance." She sighed. "I want to believe your change of heart, but you need to understand how it appears to us and how I am holding it loosely in my hands based on what I know of your father and his organization of rogue hunters."

"I understand. I'm leaving anyway, so you won't have to worry about it."

"Don't go to him. Go anywhere else, but don't go back to him, Hollis," Macy begged of her.

"If I don't, he might still try to find you. At least if I go to him, I have a chance at distracting him from Havenwood Falls." Hollis placed her hands on her hips and looked out behind them at the fantastic view of the town and the surrounding mountains. "This place is special, and it, and you, deserve the chance to be free from Dante Blackstone."

"So do you," a male voice said.

"Ryne," Hollis breathed with surprise and a tinge of hope as he approached them.

Hollis noted Macy standing uncomfortably to the side, her eyes shifting to each of them and back again. "I'm going to check in with my parents. Come say goodbye when you're ready, Hollis. They'll want to see you out of town."

Hollis nodded but didn't take her eyes from Ryne's. She hesitated. She'd hurt him, and she didn't know how to fix it. She'd never had a friendship like his, never had feelings for anyone she wanted to get close to before. As she studied him and looked deep into his eyes, she felt within herself something she'd never thought she could have. She wanted what the other Blackstones had—family, friends, and a home. She wanted a new life, and she wanted to redefine herself. Hollis wanted that life with Ryne.

"I think I love you," she blurted out. Then quickly she backpedaled with her hand over her mouth and shock on her face. "I thought that was in my head. I mean, I want you. I want this." She gestured out at the town behind them. "I want a home where I can get closer to you. I do . . . I love you." Her voice grew in confidence the more she spoke and the more she felt as she allowed herself.

"Hollis—"

"I've never felt this way before. I've never felt the way *you* make me feel. Being around you makes me happy." She smiled as she spoke.

"Hollis." Ryne's voice grew strong and stern, causing Hollis to stop. She noticed him, truly noticed him, and realized he wasn't reciprocating.

"Oh god, you don't feel the same." She put her hands to her head and turned away from him. Her heart sunk like a lead weight to her feet. "I need to go. I'm sorry, Ryne. So sorry for all I put you through. I didn't mean to hurt you. I wanted to tell you everything, but was afraid you'd hate me."

Hollis stormed past him. He reached out and grabbed her arm, stopping her, but she refused to look at him.

"Hollis." His voice was low, pained but filled with desire just the same. Hollis stared at him straight on then, seeking something worth fighting for in his eyes. When she found it, she couldn't turn away from him.

"Hollis," he whispered once more. "I can't deny the powerful pull I feel to you. It's almost like . . ." He frowned and shook his head.

"Like what?"

"It's not possible, but it's almost like I'm responding to you like you're my mate."

"Mate?" Hollis reared her head back, confused by the terminology. "Witches don't have mates," she said out loud, forgetting they hadn't talked about that part of him yet.

"You know?" Ryne's face widened with surprise, then he remembered. "Right. You're a witch hunter, so you can, what . . . sense witches?"

Hollis nodded, uncertain about saying anything more. She didn't want to break the tenuous connection they had at the moment.

"You knew and you still hung out with me. Did it not bother you? I heard it can be painful."

Hollis gave him a snarky smile. "I have excellent control."

Ryne laughed, alleviating some of the tension between them. "Truth?"

"It's true I have been trained to control all my hunter instincts. But with you, I didn't feel compelled to even try to control it. I mean, I can sense you're only half witch, so the magical energy wasn't as strong as, say, Addie's. But even so, what I did feel seemed to bring me closer to you. I wanted to be with you. I've never felt that way before, Ryne. With who I am . . . it shouldn't be possible either."

"Maybe it's true. You could be my mate," Ryne wondered aloud. He pulled her in closer to his chest and gently touched her forehead, tracing his finger over the scar she had hidden beneath her hair, and frowned.

"Ryne, what is your other half? I mean, I don't have any right to ask . . ." Hollis had the decency to look sheepish.

"Phoenix. I'm half witch and half phoenix, Hollis. Have you ever heard of such a thing?" He laughed, but it wasn't one of humor, instead more of the exasperation of an old topic of discussion he'd grown tired of. "I'm a phoenix witch who can't control either side of my powers."

Hollis hadn't ever heard of that combination of supernatural, but as she thought of it, it made sense. "I could see that. I've seen sparks of fire in your eyes when you didn't know I was looking. I'm not able to discern more than witch magic, but I knew there was more to you than human."

Ryne reached for her hand and clasped it. "Will you sit with me by the water and talk?"

She nodded, and he pulled her toward a large boulder they could both fit on.

"I'm sorry, Ryne. I'm sorry for lying to you. I'm used to keeping to the shadows and hiding, to playing a part so much, I don't even truly know who I am anymore . . . if I ever did." Hollis gazed longingly up at the falls. "I wish I did. Maybe I could be someone you deserve, someone you could love in time."

Ryne laughed and shook his head.

"What the hell are you laughing at?" Hollis frowned at him with a glare. *How dare he laugh when I'm being my most vulnerable.* This was why she shouldn't be vulnerable.

"Don't be sore, Hollis. You owe it to me to hear me out." He squeezed her hand and wouldn't let go when she tried to pull away.

"Fine."

"I'm only laughing because you are so blind." His words were almost rough, frustrated he had to spell it out. "I fell in love with you the first time we hung out. I was instantly attracted to you. I felt an undeniable pull to be near you. I even tried to stay away but I couldn't, even when you tried so hard to push me away." He laughed again. "I knew from the beginning you were hiding something, but most of all I knew you needed me." He winked at her, and she punched him in the shoulder, at which he laughed more. "You needed someone to push you and pull you out of yourself to see the bigger picture . . . to see who you could be without all the constraints you put on yourself . . . to see you the way I see you can be." Ryne turned her toward him, and with his other hand, he gently brushed some of her dark hair out of her face. "It only hurt so much to find out the way I did about your secret and your lies because I love you."

He gazed at her face, waiting for the words to sink in. When they did, Hollis's eyes brightened, and she even dared to smile.

"You love me? Even after everything you found out? Even knowing who I really am and why I came?" She couldn't help the hope that snuck into her voice.

"I do." He leaned forward and tenderly kissed the tip of her nose. She closed her eyes and leaned her head forward, touching his forehead, simply breathing him in for the moment . . . knowing the moment wouldn't last.

"Tell me about you, Ryne. How are you half witch and half phoenix? I want to know everything."

"Well, it started with my father being full phoenix and my mother being full witch. Do I really need to go into how that all happened?"

She slugged his arm again and pulled back, crossing her legs and getting more comfortable on the boulder. "Ha. Ha. No, I think I got that part figured out."

"Well, it's pretty simple. My mother was the only witch in the phoenix clan my father was from. The clans are usually pretty small. Many years ago, the clan leader had found a way to harness a witch's power to enhance his phoenix powers, thus raising him above all the others to keep his status as leader. Over time it became a clan secret to keep a witch around, but they were not to touch her. She was sacred, though a captive held against her will. My father was the clan leader's son, and he fell in love with the witch."

Hollis gasped, entranced by his story.

"He wasn't supposed to, but he did. There were grave consequences, even for the leader's son, if anyone took the witch either against her will or even with her consent. She, in turn, fell in love with him. They had a secret affair for many years until she could no longer hide she was with child—me—and my father tried to secret her away from the clan, but they found out."

"Oh no!" Hollis covered her mouth with her hand.

"My grandfather, the clan leader, put my father in solitary confinement as a punishment until I was born. He could have had him killed, but thankfully he didn't. My mother was punished as well. After she had me, she was expected to fulfill more than her duties to the clan and had to give more and more magic. It wore her down. My father noticed and tried to plead with the clan leader to back off. They weren't allowed to marry, but my father took care of her the best he could. A few years ago, my father was making another appeal to his father to free my mom, and several of the other members got riled up and even challenged my father. It was fair to do this, but he never made it to the fight. Phoenix aren't known for controlling their tempers, and several lashed out and challenged my father. If he had made it to the fight, he would have won. He was the next strongest in the clan. But they trapped him and turned him over to a group of rocs who killed him."

Hollis' eyes filled with emotion. She placed her hand on his knee. "What happened? What's a roc?"

"I'll get to the rocs. My grandfather protected us for a while, but he was getting on in years even though phoenix live a long time. I was technically next in line, but I wasn't ready to take over. My phoenix power and my witch power were in conflict, and I messed up a lot of things. Phoenix powers are connected to emotions, and mine were all over the place. In general I was a more laid-back guy than I should have been, according to the others. I had a dream they were going to kill my mom, and the next day, I left my grandfather a note and packed us up. We left. That was a couple years ago. We traveled around for a time, but eventually found our way here the end of last summer. The guy you saw me reacting to in the square the other day was a roc. A roc is essentially a giant eagle. A single flap of its enormous wing can create cyclone-type gusts of wind, and his tongue is long and forked like a snake. His kind are enemies with the phoenix because they've been jealous they don't have healing abilities or immortality, and it's tough to overcome such ingrained ancient prejudices. They are the only creatures known who can kill a phoenix."

"Wow, I had no idea phoenix, and now these roc people, were so violent. I had only heard of phoenix in stories," Hollis commented.

"Make no mistake, this is not phoenix across the board. From what I understand, other clans aren't like that. In fact, there's another phoenix in town I'd like you to meet sometime; she's a bit younger than us, and I've come to think of her like a little sister. I met her shortly after I moved here. Her name is Ember, and she's a pistol—I think you'd like her. She didn't know any others like us even existed." He paused for some air. "Anyway, I think my clan corrupted their powers by taking advantage of witch magic, and the power made them unstable and aggravated."

After a moment, he turned his gaze up at the falls. His eyes filled with emotion, and he pulled in a tight breath. "My mom was finally able to refresh her powers and be rejuvenated by the other witches in town. Havenwood Falls saved her life, and I suppose mine as well. I don't think our clan would have let us survive much longer. But she left a few months ago and hasn't checked in for quite some time. The last I heard from her, she mentioned meeting someone, which I found odd because she's never been interested in another relationship since my father. I'm a little worried something's wrong, but with her powers restored, I know she can take care of herself. Plus she's not too good with cell phones, and you've experienced the kind of reception we get up here." Ryne chuckled but added, "I miss her though. I hope she comes home soon. I'd love for you to meet her."

"Ryne! I'm so sorry. Here I've been so concerned with myself. If there's anything I can do, let me know."

He placed his hand on her knee. "Thank you," he said quietly.

Hollis was suddenly struck. "You haven't learned to use your phoenix powers because you're afraid you're corrupted, aren't you?"

Ryne looked away, shame coloring his expression, and a fire sparked in his eye. He gave her a curt nod and confirmed her suspicion. "I tried once to combine the two, and it went very wrong. I'm able to separate the witch side more easily because my mother was able to teach me, but the phoenix side is unpredictable. It tends to erupt more when my temper rises or due to fear."

"You are more powerful than you know. I can sense that much and see it in your eyes. Because you care." Hollis moved away from the boulder and sighed.

"What is it?"

"I have to leave, Ryne. I wish now more than ever before that I didn't. But I do."

Ryne slid his body up against hers and pulled her close to his chest. He inhaled in the crook of her neck, sending chills down to her toes. "Don't go, Hollis. We can find a way to protect you and misdirect your father. Please, don't go."

She turned into him and let him claim her lips. Passion grew between them. Hollis had never felt such closeness and such instant heat. She'd been caught up in the moment before, had even used her wiles to get what she needed done on a job, but never before had she felt connected with another person like their souls belonged together. Ryne kissed her like he would never see her again. His mouth roamed from hers and moved down her jawline to her neck.

"Can we go somewhere? I just want to be with you before I go," Hollis said with a breathy tone between his kisses.

He grabbed her hand, and they walked away from the falls. They didn't get far before the phone in Hollis's back pocket rang. She frowned. "You've got to be kidding. It's like he knows."

"Who?"

"My father."

CHAPTER 14

"*D*ad, have you arrived already?" Hollis asked, straight to the point. She stopped moving. "You are? Why lie to me?" Hollis frowned. Then a vacant expression crossed her face. "*What? Why did you never tell me about this?*" Looking down at her wrist, she touched the underside, then poked and prodded at it.

Ryne moved in close to her, concern written on his face. He reached for her wrist and examined it himself. Hollis could feel the color in her face drain completely out. "Why the game if you knew where I was the whole time?"

Ryne stood straight and crossed his arms, pushing his chest out. His eyes ringed with red. She wanted to smile at his show of concern, but she knew he was no match for her father . . . at least not yet.

"I'll meet you in town when you arrive and show you myself." She paused and breathed in slowly through her nose, as if trying not to lose her patience. "It's no big deal at all, Dad. I'll just meet you." Another pause. "See you then. Bye." She hung up.

Ryne gripped her elbow, probably attempting to steady her. Hollis felt light on her feet.

"What was that about?" he asked.

"He knows. Somehow he knows." Hollis studied her wrist and poked and prodded a part of it.

He moved his head in closer to see what she looked at. "What are you doing?"

"I can't even see it."

"Hollis! What?"

"A tracker. He put a damn tracker in my wrist. He's known where I was or at least approximately, since signal up here is spotty, where I—or Havenwood Falls—was this whole time. I can't believe he fucking tracked me!" Her voice grew as did her eyes with each statement she made. "Do you have a knife?" She looked up at Ryne with panic.

"No way in hell am I giving you a knife! You want to cut it out of you? You don't even know where it is or how big it is." Ryne tried for a voice of reason when he realized she wasn't even listening. "We should ask the Blackstones and the Luna Coven. Maybe they can find it with magic, see what we're dealing with."

Hollis nodded absently. "Yeah, okay. Good idea."

Hollis didn't even remember Ryne putting her into his truck and taking her to the Blackstone home in Havenwood Heights. Luckily, they didn't have far to go from the falls.

"Are you ready to leave?" Macy asked as she came out the manor's front door, followed closely by Lilith and Letitia.

"She's not leaving. At least not yet," Ryne supplied for her.

"Why not?" Lilith asked, crossing her arms over her chest. Her blond hair whipped in her face as she swung around, accentuating the tightness in the lines of her face.

No one said anything, and the tension grew.

"Do you want me to tell them?" Ryne asked her quietly.

"Well, for the goddess's sake, someone tell us what's going on," Lilith demanded.

Hollis stepped forward. "He's getting closer."

"Then you should be on your way," Lilith dryly suggested.

"Perhaps there is more to this story, dear," Letitia said, paying closer attention.

Hollis stuck out her arm. "He tracked me. I didn't know about it, I swear. I don't know how well it's worked up here in the mountains, but it has at least given him a good idea where we are. He played me the whole time. I think he knows . . . knew I would switch . . . I don't know. I don't know anything anymore."

"I see," was all Lilith said, staring at Hollis's bared wrist.

Macy approached her. "I'll call Gallad and see if his grandmother has a way to magically find the tracker or stop it or get it out? I'm not sure what she can do, but I'll ask."

Hollis nodded and offered a small smile to Macy. "Thank you." She would have been embarrassed by how weak her voice sounded, but she was still in too much shock to care.

"We'll wait for the Augustines inside." Letti ushered them all into the house and out of view of the neighbors.

Not more than ten minutes later, a knock sounded at the door.

A tall, handsome young man walked in like he owned the place with a crooked smile on his face as soon as he saw Macy. She ran into his arms, and he planted a big kiss on her cheek.

"Thank you for coming." She looked to the older woman, whom Hollis had seen at the Court—Mathilde, she thought the woman's name was. "Thank you, Mathilde," Macy supplied.

"Of course, dear. Now what seems to be the trouble?" She looked from Macy to Hollis.

"Dante placed a tracker in my wrist. I didn't know about it, and the reception seems to be spotty based on the way he spoke—he didn't seem to have an exact location yet. But then again, he could be lying about that too, and maybe he's on his way up the mountain now." Hollis rushed her words out with frustration and defeat.

Mathilde held out her hand. "Let me see, Hollis."

"Can't we just cut it out and be done with it?" she impatiently asked.

Mathilde's eyes went wide, but then considered what she said. "Even with magic, that wouldn't be our best option. Let's save that for a last resort."

She patted Hollis's hand then clasped it between her own. She closed her eyes and hummed something low and indecipherable. The room grew heavy with anticipation. Gallad moved up next to them and, keeping his hands in the air, he positioned one below and one above his grandmother's hands, adding his own energy and magic to her spell.

Quickly glancing around, Hollis noted the Blackstones stepped back, allowing the witches to do their work but also preventing the magic from bothering them too much. Hollis could feel the magical energy building around her to the point it began to do more than agitate her. Just before she closed her eyes to shut out the room and focus her breathing on the pain, she noticed a ring on Mathilde's finger—a shiny opalescent stone that illuminated with the increase of power.

Hollis cried out and practically collapsed with the surge of power as it flooded her body. She felt hands behind her, holding her up. Macy and Letti both uttered soft words of encouragement and strength. She knew the power must cause them pain as well, but they still joined to help her.

"I can do no more," Mathilde breathed heavily, and beads of sweat shimmered at the sides of her face. She grasped Gallad's offered arm to steady herself. "I'm afraid it has been bound by another witch's spell. It's not that I'm not powerful enough, but the spell is complicated and twisted. Like a labyrinth of layers entangled together. It would take a tremendous amount of energy and time, which we do not have."

Hollis breathed in deep and nodded. "Thank you for trying. I'll leave right away and hope the connection has been spotty."

"Wait, just a moment, dear," Mathilde continued. "What I did do was put a spell around it that should work like a shield and buy us some more time to find a more permanent solution." Her eyes, aged and wise, peered into Hollis's eyes. "I'm assuming you want to stay?"

Hollis looked around the room at each of the Blackstones, the witches, and finally Ryne. She did want to stay.

"I won't put you all in danger. This is on me. Thank you for shielding the tracker. That will give me time to relocate far away in the event it comes back online. Dante will find me somewhere else, far from here."

"No," Ryne interjects. "That's not good enough! There has to be another option so you can stay."

"I don't deserve to stay here and build a life like nothing ever happened. I—" Hollis was cut off by the shrill ring of someone's phone.

Mathilde answered her phone and frowned. "I'm with them now. We'll get prepared. Thank you, Sheriff." She hung up and looked to Lilith.

"Dante has been spotted in Durango. We need access below Soothing Sips, Lilith. Is Brock there now?"

Lilith placed her hands on her waist and nodded. "I'll get him prepared."

Lilith took out her own phone and walked out of the room.

"See, even more reason for me to go to him now," Hollis pleaded. "There will be others with Dante. They're not all bad and shouldn't be included. They've been my family this far, and I don't want them hurt. I'll go to him and try to get them to turn back." She took a deep breath. "If he won't, then you can intervene."

"I'll go with you, then," Ryne said with determination.

"Why don't you use the magical dust you used before to confuse their minds and send them away from the mountain like last time when he followed me back?" Macy asked. It was at that moment Hollis realized why Macy had been so hard on her: because she still carried her own guilt for almost bringing Dante to the borders of Havenwood Falls.

Letti shook her head. "He'll be expecting that possibility and probably come prepared to combat it." Letti frowned, then looked to Mathilde. "Seems Dante may be using witch magic to fight witch magic."

Mathilde also frowned but nodded in agreement. "I was considering the same thing. For him to have such magic around the tracker, and to be so close so fast, he would have to be working with or somehow harnessing a witch's magic. And that is an entirely different concern."

"Indeed," Letti concurred. She turned to Hollis. "Do you know of any witches who would work with your father?"

"With his reputation for killing them all? No way. I've never seen a witch with him or even felt one at any of our homes." Hollis frowned in thought. "There have been times more recently when he wouldn't let any of us go with him to 'check on something'," she said, using air quotes. "I suppose it's possible he keeps one somewhere. It would have to be against their will, though. No way any witch would voluntarily work with him unless he held something pretty big over their heads."

"That's what I was afraid of," Letti said sadly.

"Time to go," Lilith directed as she re-entered the room. She had even taken a moment to change from her business attire into dark cargo pants with plenty of pockets, a tight black T-shirt, and a jacket. With her bright blond hair in its sharp A-line cut, Lilith looked the part of a badass ready to battle. "Everyone meet at the armory."

"You have an armory?" Hollis offered a fierce smile. She could appreciate someone ready for a fight at a moment's notice. To protect this town, she assumed the supernatural residents had to be prepared for anything that may come their way.

Lilith turned her head toward Hollis and gave her a smile that sent chills down her back. "You know it. We protect our own, Hollis." She walked out the door.

Macy sidled up to Hollis. "If you stick around, that includes you, Hollis. I'm sorry I was so hard on you before. I hope you stay."

CHAPTER 15

*B*ack on the east side of the town square, just a half block away from Whisper Falls Inn, Hollis watched several people enter Soothing Sips. She recognized a couple from the Court, but even more had arrived. Hollis sat with Ryne in his truck, taking a moment for themselves.

"Ryne, I don't want you to join the fight."

"You've got to be kidding me! Is this because my power is weak?" he asked, suddenly dejected.

"Of course not!" She turned to look him straight in the eyes. "Your power is anything but weak. But you're part witch, and I don't want anything to happen to you. If there's any way for my father to know how I feel about you, he will target you to teach me a lesson." She paused. "It wouldn't be the first time."

Ryne grabbed her hand and brought it to his lips. He kissed each of her knuckles while watching her, his eyes boring into her own.

"Ryne." She started to say something but got lusciously distracted watching him kiss her skin. He chuckled, then stopped.

"I want more time with you," she whispered. "I just found you."

"We'll get that time, I promise. You're my mate, Hollis Blackstone, and I plan on keeping you."

Hollis offered him a small smile. She wished with all her heart that could be true. Unfortunately, she just didn't know if it would.

"Let's go inside before they plan this without me," Hollis said, and she reached for the door handle.

"I'm going with you, and I'll be by your side." He stared her down. "Don't even try to do this on your own, Hollis. You may be a badass fighter, but I can hold my own even without magic." He jokingly flexed his muscles.

"I believe you can." She smiled and nodded. "Together."

They entered Soothing Sips, a rustically modern tasting room for the Stone Falls Winery. Hollis couldn't help but appreciate the simple wood, metal, and concrete decor. Plentiful bottles of wine were expertly displayed against the wall, behind the long concrete countertop. She decided she'd come back with Ryne after whatever happened, happened. She hoped she would have the opportunity, but she had to consider the fact that even if they defeated Dante, she would have to still account for her crimes and face whatever punishment the Court might dish out.

Macy and Gallad stood behind the counter, waiting for them. "Follow us. We'll show you the secret armory."

Hollis rubbed her hands together, excitement lighting her eyes. No matter what, she was a born fighter, and nothing compared to the feel of a weapon in her hands. Ryne laughed as if he could read her mind.

Hollis raised an eyebrow at him. "What?"

"Nothing. Just picturing you gripping a powerful weapon between your hands and seeing the passion rise in your eyes."

A throat cleared. "Um, weapons now. Get a room later," Macy said with an embarrassed chuckle.

"Right." Hollis licked her upper lip and winked at Ryne, suddenly feeling more free than she ever had, with the weight of her secrets lifted.

"Shit, girl. You slay me," Ryne said, and slapped her ass as she walked in front of him to follow Macy and Gallad into a back room.

Through a door into a basement, they found themselves in a

much larger space than what should be structurally available. Several people milled around and examined different weapons hanging from the wall. Hollis sucked in a sudden breath and gained control of her hunter side. Continuous tingles shot up her arms. Many of the people in the basement were powerful witches. Several were people she didn't even recognize. They all turned and stared when she walked into the room.

Mathilde got everyone's attention after Gallad whistled for them to listen up. She introduced Hollis to the room and explained that she, and the town, needed their help. She went on to explain how Dante, the rogue witch hunter, was closing in on Havenwood Falls with the intent to attack. His main objective was the witches, so they were to fight in pairs or groups.

"Lilith, direct them to the weapons, then Addie will explain the battle strategy."

Lilith stepped forward. "Many of you have been in here before. You've fought for Havenwood Falls before. Pick your weapon of choice and sign it out with Reggie at the table. He's also going to put a spelled bit of liquid magic on the tip for extra measure. Be very careful not to touch it yourself, or you'll be down for the count." She stepped back, finished.

Addie stepped forward. "Our objective is not to kill but to capture. But if killing is your last defense, by all means, protect yourself. We will be stealthy and hidden at first to assess his forces. We have reason to believe young hunters will be with him, and his way is all they know. We also have reason to believe he may have the assistance of witch magic, so be prepared for anything. This is not your usual witch hunter. He's been after our town since the 1800s, and I'd like nothing more than to put him in the Infernum for good." She paused as Sheriff Kasun approached behind her. He whispered something in her ear, and she nodded.

"Sheriff said his scouts have eyes on Dante. He's still in Montrose for now and doesn't appear to be in a hurry. Either he has a plan, or he doesn't know the direction to head in yet. This gives us a little time. Choose your weapons. Conceal them as you leave.

Some of you go out the back door. We don't want to concern the rest of the town. Tonight is the Moons in the Mist Bonfire, and the perfect cover. It also means a lot of people will be out tonight, so be discreet. Meet after nightfall at the edge of town, by Cooley Creek. We'll spread out from there, covering all access points down Miles Mountain. We're seeking Dante and his people out before they can find us. When it's all over, be sure to return your borrowed weapons. Dismissed," Addie said with militant tone and direction.

Saundra Beaumont approached Hollis once her granddaughter was finished. "Mathilde has informed me of your other little problem." She pointed to Hollis's wrist. "We will work on a permanent solution if you wish us to. I can't decide for the Court if they will permit you to stay, but would you like me to proceed either way?"

Hollis didn't answer lightly. She glanced at Ryne, who simply watched her, letting her know the decision had to be hers. "Yes, I would like you to. I understand the Court may vote against me. That's something I'll have to accept. But if there is the possibility, I'd like to stay."

Saundra nodded and left the basement.

"I'm sure she'll come up with something. She's the most powerful witch and one of three leaders of the Luna Coven, alongside Mathilde and Roman Bishop," Ryne said with complete confidence, which in turn strengthened Hollis's confidence.

"Ryne, what's the Infernum?"

Ryne shivered. "It's a part of Hell for supernaturals. When bad supes die, that's where their souls go. And those who are impossible to kill get sent there, too. Havenwood Falls has its own portal there used by the hellhounds—"

"Wait. Hellhounds are real?" Hollis interrupted.

"Yes." Ryne nodded toward a couple of big, intimidating guys dressed as bikers, standing near the exit. "I'm sure others are probably out on Dante's trail right now. They escort souls to Hell, and the Luna Coven traps others there, in like their own little slice of the Infernum. I've only heard stories about what kind of creatures have gotten themselves locked up there."

Hollis frowned. The thought of her father being locked up in an impenetrable prison in Hell sounded to be about what he deserved, but he was still her father, and she wasn't sure she could be a part of entrapping him.

"Take your pick, Hollis and Ryne," Macy said, bringing Hollis out of her thoughts. Her arms gestured wide as if the armory was an all you could eat buffet.

Hollis smiled greedily and went shopping.

CHAPTER 16

$\mathcal{J}$ ust before Hollis and Ryne were to meet the hunting party, they had a date to carry out. Ryne picked Hollis up in his truck in front of NamaStays Inn. Garbed in her tall black buckled boots, black leather pants, and black leather jacket, she felt more like her old self. However, she wore a couple new additions—new pieces—she had acquired from Callie's: a vintage V-neck Journey T-shirt that allowed her tattoos to peek out from her neck and a narrow piece of silver metal stamped with the word *Redefined* on a strip of suede hung from her neck. With her long dark hair down and blowing in the breeze, she felt wild and free, even knowing she would be hunting her own father later that night.

"Wow, you look . . . electrified!" Ryne said with hunger in his eyes, which were rimmed with red.

"Ha! You're one to talk. Do you know your eyes do that red circle thing sometimes?" she asked as she climbed in the truck.

Ryne's mouth fell open, then quickly closed before he sheepishly explained, "It happens at heightened emotional states."

"I noticed."

"You ready to see some fire?" Ryne teasingly asked.

"Let's see what your town's got!"

Ryne parked his truck along the side of the road wherever he could find a spot. It appeared the Moons in the Mist Bonfire was a town favorite. Ryne had explained the event was a way to celebrate the coming of summer, and apparently everyone was excited to bring on the new season. As they entered the large park, they were greeted by a wave of heat wafting from the largest of the bonfires. Scattered about, several smaller barrels filled with wood were being lit as well. The sun continued its descent while the moon rose high in the darkening sky. Stars, too, peeked out early from the tapestry above, hesitant still to reveal their full glory until darkness had arrived.

"This is really cool," Hollis said. Townspeople set up smaller fires for barbecues and additional heat. High schoolers threw random burnable items into the insatiable blaze of the main fire, music blared from some unseen source, and others strung beautiful white lights through the trees for a magical ambiance.

Ryne grinned from ear to ear. "It is, isn't it? I wasn't in town yet for it last year."

Hollis could see the appreciation and even desire for the fire glow in Ryne's eyes. Being a phoenix, he had told her he had an affinity for fire, but she wasn't sure to what extent.

"How does it work? Could you touch the fire and not get burned?" she whispered to him in secrecy.

Ryne glanced at those around them to be sure. "I can feel it, but yeah, I could hold it for a short bit. I played with it once when I was younger, and I think maybe my primary element as a witch is fire. But I can't engulf myself in natural fire like a full phoenix could."

"Good to know. Stay out of fires." Hollis playfully smiled.

"Come on, let's get some food before it's gone," Ryne said and grabbed her hand, tugging her toward a food table with a line of people already forming. They stayed at the bonfire, and Ryne introduced her to several of his friends, until darkness had fully fallen.

"Well, time to go," Hollis said, noting a few people from the armory already leaving the party with a nod in their direction.

"Shit," Ryne spat. "I don't want this part of tonight to end. I'm having fun with you."

Hollis reached up on her tiptoes and kissed his chin. "Me too. After it's all over, we'll have fun. I have a lifetime without fun to make up for." She winked and pulled him along behind her as they headed for his truck.

When they arrived at a trailhead by Cooley Creek, Ryne parked the truck and got out. The Blackstones were there waiting for them and accompanied Hollis and Ryne on foot to the meeting spot. Hollis was about to confront Dante, and protect the borders of Havenwood Falls—such a one-eighty from her original mission. She walked beside Lilith, who had been eerily quiet since they arrived. Brock joined the group and quietly chatted with Ryne.

"Something I'm wondering," Macy began as she jogged up in between her mother and Hollis.

"What's that, Macy?" Lilith asked almost indulgently.

"Why does Hollis have dark hair and not the typical white-blond of the witch hunters? Actually, I remember many of the rogue hunters did also. Did you dye it, Hollis?"

Hollis noticed Lilith stiffen next to her.

"Macy, this is hardly the time to talk hair," her mother reprimanded.

"No, it's always been this color," Hollis admitted. She was surprised at Macy's question, however. "Many of our hunters have dark hair. It has to do with the parents and their—" Hollis was cut off, seeing Lilith's glare of death behind Macy's head. She wondered what Lilith could be hiding, but decided to play along until a better time. "I suppose it could be due to having both parents be hunters. Which I realize is somewhat rare, as there aren't that many non-related hunters."

Hollis noted Lilith's apparent ease in the barest lowering of her shoulders. When this was over, she had questions of her own for the matriarch of the Havenwood Falls hunters. Hollis's reason seemed to appease Macy for the moment, but from what she'd observed of Macy so far, she wasn't one to let things go.

"But my brother Brice has only one hunter parent." Macy chewed over the information for a minute but didn't get the chance to continue.

The group had stopped in a darkened, quiet area just off the road on the edge of town and the forest heading down the mountain.

"Thank you all for coming," Saundra Beaumont announced. "Sheriff Kasun has been keeping me apprised of Dante's whereabouts with use of his patrols and members of the Blaekthorn pack who have pitched in, as well as Rusty Higgins and the forest services. He and a large group have spread out below Miles Mountain. We're going to split up. A leader in each group will have communication links to the leaders of the other groups and with headquarters back here, which will be myself, Mathilde Augustine, and Letitia Blackstone. The following are leaders of the groups: Addie and Tase, Michaela and Xandru, Lilith Blackstone and Roman Bishop, Brock and Reggie Blackstone, and finally Tate Kasun and Shade StormIron. Each of you will join a group. Time is of the essence."

Hollis was struck by how many people had turned out for the witch hunters' hunt. Even more than those who came to the armory showed up. Hollis couldn't understand why these people would risk their lives and be willing to fight for her mistake. But she remembered their cause was something bigger and more precious— their town.

Everyone moved quickly into what seemed like already predetermined groups. Lilith and the man Hollis had seen on the Court—Roman—approached them.

"Hollis and Ryne, you will join our group along with Macy, Gallad, and several others from the Luna Coven," Lilith directed.

Hollis nodded, willing to comply for the moment, but she had no intention of letting the newest members of her family get caught in the crossfire with her other family. She glanced up at the tall, commanding Roman Bishop. She cocked her head and studied him unabashedly. He simply stared back at her with a challenging gleam in his ocean eyes, then gave her a one-sided smile that was more sinister than cocky.

"What's your deal?" she stupidly asked.

Roman raised an eyebrow at her insipid question.

"Why are you helping me, a witch hunter? I mean, you're obviously a mage—a very powerful one—but your magic is different. It's not quite black, but it's not on the pure side either. How is it you are on the Court here?"

Roman looked down at her, his expression stony. "I have my reasons for helping. I am powerful. That's all you need to know. As for my Court position, that is for me to know."

"And me to find out?" Hollis snarkily asked.

Without answering, he turned and walked away, expecting the group to follow him. Hollis frowned after him.

"Don't poke the beast," Macy whispered. "No one truly knows—well, I'm sure Saundra or someone knows—but nobody else knows the truth about the Bishop boys. They are mysterious, and their actions border on illegal, reprehensible, and dangerous, but it's never fully proven and somehow overlooked."

"Yeah, you don't want to be on his bad side," Gallad chimed in, then smiled as if it were just another night filled with pleasant conversation.

"You all take strange to a new level here," Hollis playfully responded.

"And proud of it." Gallad stuck out his chest and beat on it like a Neanderthal.

There was something so natural about walking and talking with Macy and Gallad; it warmed her heart. Hollis was beginning to feel like she might belong.

"Keep up," Roman barked as they took a hiking path down the middle of Mount Mae.

They hiked for hours with nothing and no one in sight who shouldn't be.

"No one is out here," Roman was saying, then stopped abruptly. Hollis and the other witch hunters all froze. The place at the base of her neck that warned her when a witch hunter neared practically electrified her with how many she abruptly registered.

"He's here," Hollis whispered, looking slowly around their group. "Where is he?"

"You don't have to whisper." Roman sighed. "I've placed a silencing spell around us, and cloaked us in a shield of invisibility," he dryly supplied.

Hollis nodded in appreciation. "Nice." She peered out into the darkness of the forest. The chirps and sounds of the nightlife had silenced. Her father's presence deafened even the creatures of the night. "I don't see him yet, but he's out there. I can feel him."

They continued a bit farther. Ryne held Hollis's hand and squeezed it every time she paused to listen or send out her hunter senses. She squeezed his back, though she couldn't look him in the eyes. Her most recent decision weighed heavily upon her heart. She only waited for the right opportunity.

Lilith continuously glanced her way out of the corner of her eye. She had to know. Hollis tried not to catch her eye, but kept her gaze outward into the forest. A twig snapped behind them, and they all spun around. Several of Dante's rogues approached them from behind. She sucked in a sharp gust of air. She hadn't realized how it might affect her to see Nala, Rachel, and Charlie—people she grew up with and considered family—hunting *her*, or at least the people she had become fond of. Macy came up alongside her and threaded her arm through Hollis's in what she could only assume was a show of solidarity. Hollis patted Macy's hand, but pulled away as the rogues moved closer.

Vaguely she heard Lilith talking to someone on her phone, letting them know how many they found in their area and they suspected Dante wasn't far behind them.

Hollis tuned all the excess noise out when she saw her father come out from behind a large tree. Though his back was to her, the air rushed out of her lungs. Hollis's hand flew to her chest as she steadied her breathing. Even knowing he couldn't see them, the thought of him being so close to Ryne and the other witches, especially, caused her to realize just how much she had grown to love them in such a short amount of time. Anger rose in her chest and colored her cheeks. Her fists clenched at her sides. She had to do something.

Hollis stepped forward, about to cross the boundary of Roman's magic shield protecting them from sight. Someone grabbed her elbow and kept her from advancing. Ryne. She knew he wouldn't understand.

"Wait." But the voice didn't belong to Ryne. It belonged to Lilith Blackstone. Hollis turned and frowned.

"I know you want to let me go," Hollis whispered under her breath. "You're hiding something, and I am someone who could shed light. So just let me go."

Lilith tugged harder, pulling Hollis back into her shoulder. "You don't know what you're doing. I know the power Dante can wield against your mind even without magic. I can't let you." Hollis shot a look at Lilith's face and was surprised to see guilt and shame and even fear in the woman's eyes. Lilith held up her phone. "Plus Saundra called. They have a solution to your tracker issue and an idea to send Dante away. But she needs a little more time."

Hollis bit her lip and nodded in understanding. "Okay. I can give her a little more time." She looked into Lilith's blue eyes, silently pleading with her. "Can you trust me?"

Lilith hesitated, then nodded. She glanced to the side, where the others stood studying the advancing rogue hunters with weapons out, ready for anything to happen, including Ryne. "He's not going to like it."

"No, he's not." And with that, Hollis didn't hesitate. She turned from Lilith and the team and took a step beyond the protection of Roman's spell. Ryne yelled for her to stop. She glanced back at him just barely in time to see Roman and Gallad holding him back. Ryne's eyes rimmed red and started to glow, just as she felt the snap of magic against her skin as she fully crossed the line.

Hollis quickly pulled herself together and sauntered toward the man she called father. After all, she was a badass assassin, trained by one of the best.

"Hello, Father."

CHAPTER 17

"*I* thought you were going to let me know when you arrived, Father. Let me give you the info I collected." Hollis stood behind him with her arms crossed, looking every bit the part of the assassin he would have last seen her as.

Dante slowly turned around with a closed smile on his face. "Hollis, you don't seem too surprised to see me." He scanned the area surrounding her. "In fact, I'm willing to wager you brought some new friends with you. Though how you are concealing them . . ." Then his face lit up sarcastically. "Witches, is it? So you've turned against me, have you? And I thought you were the one I could trust."

"Yet, you didn't really, did you?" Hollis held out her wrist, fury filling her eyes.

Dante shrugged, unconcerned at her outburst. "I need to keep track of my assets." He pulled down the edges of his black leather jacket and straightened his collar. "I'm guessing Lilith is with you around here somewhere . . . and perhaps even young Macy. I had high hopes for her once, too. Oh well." Again he shrugged.

"Leave them out of this," Hollis said, keeping up a casual façade on the outside, though inside a storm brewed. "Dad, I just wanted to tell you you're wrong about the other Blackstones and about the witches—at least most witches. They aren't all bad, and they don't deserve to die just because they were born with extra gifts they didn't ask for."

Dante's face was a mask of apathy except for his eyes. His eyes grew flat and filled with the prospect of death. "So then, you've chosen them over me."

Hollis almost felt sorry for him. "No, Dad. I've chosen a different way of life for myself. I don't want to be an assassin anymore. I want to settle down and have a family of my own. I can't do that with the life I have with you."

"Of course you can. Don't be stupid," he spat, taking a step toward her. "I did. I had you and others, didn't I?"

Hollis pursed her lips in frustration. "I don't want to hunt witches. I don't want to kill witches anymore."

"After everything I have done for you? After everything I gave you, you're going to throw it all away, just like that?" His voice remained the same level the entire time. The tactic was more intimidating than if he had been yelling.

"I need to try something different. I hope you can let me go." Hollis began slowly taking one step at a time backward the way she came, hoping to reach the shield barrier—if it was even still there. If they left her to deal with Dante on her own, she was as good as dead. And she wouldn't even blame them.

Dante advanced toward her, malicious intent now deeply etched into his face. She hadn't seen him truly angry in a long time. His calm demeanor hiding anger underneath the surface terrified most of them, but when he teetered on the verge of an unstable burst of rage, he was truly scary.

Hollis took several more steps in retreat. She knew better than to run from a predator; she refused to be the prey. She knew better than to run from her father; her lessons had taught her to hold her own. She had to stand up to him, but she didn't think she could handle his rage on her own this time.

"Dad, please let this go. It's time to move on. Let the Blackstones alone and leave it in the past. Marie is dead and gone. I saw her grave."

"I won't ever let this go!" His eyes glossed over as he shouted. "My sister betrayed our family! She turned her back on who we are —who she was supposed to be! Don't you get it? Her descendants need the chance to experience the fullness of being witch hunters! They've been deceived and lied to, kept hidden from their gifts and denied their power." He beat his fists against his chest as he continued to advance. "I can give that to them!" He looked wildly about. "Do you hear me, Lilith Blackstone? You are holding your children back." He turned in a circle with his arms spread wide as if taunting her to face him. "It's their birthright to experience the power killing a witch gives them! You know better!"

Hollis took advantage of his rage-induced distraction and felt the sizzle of the magical shield border behind her, but he spun to see her face. His own was a sudden mask of indifference except for the glimpse of cold hatred in his eyes.

"Goodbye, Father. I've found a place and a people with whom I can be loved for who I am. Don't look for me."

She took the final step and disappeared behind the magical shield. A relief she didn't know existed lifted off her shoulders and she stood taller. Lighter. And though she smiled, a single tear for the loss of her past trickled down her cheek. She would allow no more than that; she made her choice.

On the other side of the shield, Dante held his head up and jutted out his chin. He would not be made a fool, and Hollis knew it.

"Kill anyone you find," he instructed his rogues now closing in around him. Dante didn't take his eyes off the place Hollis had just stood. She could feel the hatred within his eyes bore straight into her soul. Hollis turned from the edge and found the loving eyes of Ryne searching her face. And she ran to him and let him embrace her like no one ever had. He escorted her away from the space.

"You shouldn't have gone out there alone. We were supposed to do this together," he whispered roughly in her ear. She could feel the frustrated fear in his tone and laid her head on his shoulder.

"I'm sorry," she whispered in return, "I needed to face him first on my own." The others moved in behind her, surrounding her with support. She knew Lilith stood at the edge, staring Dante down, could feel her energy spiking as if Lilith wanted to run out and fight Dante herself.

Only a moment later, she watched Roman grip Lilith's elbow and tug her along with the rest, out of the vicinity of the rogue Blackstones. Saundra Beaumont, Mathilde Augustine, a man and a woman about Hollis's age, and a young witch barely out of high school crested the hillside above them. Saundra and Mathilde, though both getting on in their years, looked fierce, and the essence of magic surged powerfully in and around them. Hollis could feel it creep along her skin like electricity. The man and woman in their twenties felt human for all Hollis could tell, and the other witch, though young in years, had a powerful streak to her magic she had not yet learned how to fully temper, based on the vibes of energy Hollis received. They stepped inside the protective shield with an audible *snap*. Saundra spotted Dante over their shoulders and then swiveled to pierce Hollis with her all-too-knowing gaze.

"Hollis, we have found a solution to your tracker," she said.

Hollis held out her wrist. "Anything. What can you do?"

Saundra gestured back to the man behind her. He was tall though of a slight build, dark, and handsome, complete with a scruffy beard. Hollis wondered if he was supposed to be some kind of bodyguard, though he was casual in appearance with his denim jacket, ripped jeans, and boots.

"This is Montezuma Tayute." The man stepped up next to the witch. "He is also a technological master among other things. And he has an idea that might work, since your tracker involves magic and high tech machinery."

Hollis listened as Montezuma quickly explained the gist of what he would do.

"Call me Monte. First, we can try to remove it, but based on what Mathilde told me, it is tied to your essence."

At Hollis's look of confusion, Saundra cut in. "If we remove it, there's a chance it could kill you."

Hollis's eyes grew wide with surprise. "Oh."

"With a little tech and a little magic provided by Saundra, I can hack into the device and reroute the signal to bounce from satellite to satellite and confuse the signal so it's always in a different location around the world while she is prying into the other spell surrounding the tracker."

"Wow, you can do that?" Hollis was afraid to hope the idea was possible.

"I can." Monte confidently stated, though his demeanor was almost too relaxed for Hollis's comfort.

"I'll be assisting Montezuma with magic to enhance his technical skills. The Luna Coven has also agreed to offer you a spell to conceal your life's essence, but you'd be bound to Havenwood Falls," Saundra explained with grave sincerity. "Or you could walk away and go anywhere you want, but I fear your father could still trace your essence eventually."

Hollis paused. She looked up into Ryne's hopeful eyes and knew she was home. "I choose to stay here."

Saundra nodded. "Montezuma will disable the tracker right here so your signal doesn't give anything away." She gestured with her head toward Dante and the others, who still scoured the mountainside. Even though they moved farther away, time was of the essence. "The rest we will take care of tomorrow with the Court of the Sun and the Moon."

Hollis followed Saundra's gaze, watching as Dante hiked up an incline just on the other side of where they stood. "How will we get him to leave? Do we fight?"

"No, dear, I think that won't be necessary tonight," Mathilde explained. "That's what Liberty Veitch and Circe Alexander are here for. Liberty is a distraction, and Circe is skilled with illusions."

Hollis frowned, but nodded at the women, accepting their help.

She imagined Liberty was a distraction in most settings with her generous curves snug as a glove in her tight leathers. She was otherworldly beautiful, but Hollis didn't think that the woman's appearance would be an appropriate distraction for what they were doing.

Dante held out his phone and looked at what Hollis guessed was her tracking signal, and he turned back toward them.

"Hurry! Do it, Monte!" She held out her wrist to him, not caring what he had to do to her.

He simply held her wrist, lowering them both to the ground so he could crouch down with his bag. He pulled out some kind of tablet and a small device hooked to a cable he connected to the tablet. Monte looked up at her. "Okay, this might sting a bit."

Hollis looked him in the eyes, daring him to continue warning her. "Do it."

Monte gave her a toothy grin. "Yes, ma'am."

He placed his thumb over the place where the tracker supposedly was and held the small device against her skin. Saundra came up behind him and placed her hand on his shoulder. Hollis could feel the magic flow from the witch while Monte's other hand flew over the tablet, tapping and sliding across the screen. He then mumbled something under his breath Hollis thought sounded like "Please work."

She felt a prick in her skin and then a flood of intensely local energy pierce through her wrist. She struggled not to cry out, it was so intense. Ryne came up behind her and placed his hands on her shoulders, giving her a squeeze.

"All done," Monte abruptly said and packed up his stuff.

Hollis held her wrist to her chest then pulled away to examine her arm. She was sure there would be blood or something, but her skin didn't even look marred. Not even a scratch.

"Wow. A sting, huh?" She looked up at Monte with a raised eyebrow.

He winked at her and shrugged. "Knew you could handle it."

"All done then?" Ryne asked, helping her to her feet then also examining her wrist, though there was nothing to see.

"All done."

Hollis watched as Dante tossed his phone with frustration to one of his rogues next to him. His eyes scanned the area around them, sure he could see something else. Unexpectedly, he turned around and walked away. Though confused at how easily he was giving up, Hollis breathed a sigh of relief and turned to Saundra.

"Thank you. And thank you, Monte."

"Hollis! Look out!" Macy screamed.

Time seemed to stand still as Hollis turned. A dagger flew toward her in what felt like slow motion. Directly behind it stood her father with his arm extended, having released the dagger, with a cruel sneer on his face. She knew it would be a direct hit. While the magical barrier they stood behind shielded their location and muted their voices, it would do nothing against a physical weapon striking through it.

"NO!" Ryne yelled. He threw himself in front of Hollis and across the magical barrier. Ryne took the hit, having knocked her to the ground in the process, partially across the barrier. Hollis screamed but could see nothing but a burst of light combined with sparks of red and orange before she and everyone else was plunged into the darkness of night.

CHAPTER 18

"*R*yne!" Hollis called out in a panic, jumping up off the ground. She had no idea if he was hit or how bad it was. Just as quickly as the light had erupted then left, an orange glow surrounded the figure of a man hunched over.

"Ryne?" Hollis whispered, half in awe and half in concern for him. He'd accessed his power, and she knew he didn't think he could control it. He seemed pretty in control at the moment to her. In fact, he seemed powerful and even stronger than before. He stood forcefully up with power rushing through him. Throwing his arms back, he released a transparent image of a phoenix that hovered above him. From her position behind him, she watched in awe as magical fiery red wings transposed over his back. He hadn't become the phoenix—he had embodied the spirit of one; maybe the result of his combined heritage.

Dante stared at Ryne with a dawning familiarity and possibly a hint of fear. "You must be Ryne Calloway."

"I am," Ryne growled with an inhuman sound.

"Does she belong to you?" Dante asked, looking nowhere but at Ryne. Hollis wanted to rebuke her father, to say that she belonged to no one but herself, but out from behind a tree Nala brought forward a disheveled woman—a witch from the tingles racing up Hollis's arms—with her wrists bound as if a prisoner. Oh no.

"Mom? Mom!" Ryne shouted with a tremor to his voice, barely containing the power he held.

"Dad? A witch? What are you doing?" Hollis asked as all the air fled her lungs. She couldn't believe what she was seeing. The culmination of everything she had believed about her father shattered before her eyes with this final revelation. Her father had not only consorted with a witch, but he kidnapped Ryne's mother.

Dante shrugged. "She was easy and unassuming prey. I needed her power to accomplish a few things, and her knowledge of Havenwood Falls came in handy too."

Hollis felt sick. She knew her father well and was sure he had tortured the poor woman for information, or at the very least had threatened her son in order to gain her cooperation. "Oh, Ryne, I had no idea. I'm so sorry."

From behind Ryne, she could only guess his eyes glowed orange. And in his hands he held what looked like white glowing orbs of light.

"Ryne, you have to believe me. I had no idea."

Ryne crossed his arms in an "X" at his chest then flung them outward, releasing the white light as it extended behind him in a line in front of the others. It erupted in flames, creating a protective barrier behind him, keeping Hollis contained with the others and out of harm's reach. Ryne stepped forward so nothing stood between him and Dante but space.

"No one hurts my family!" Ryne shouted, the pain of his past combined with the hope of his future filtering through. Ryne cocked back his hand, filled once more with orbs of crackling white light, ready to launch his attack back at Dante.

"Ryne," Hollis called to him. She couldn't let him follow through. She would find a way to rescue his mom. When he didn't respond, she called again louder. "Ryne," she pleaded, "we'll find a way!"

She wanted to see Dante punished just as much as the rest of them after he tried to kill her, but she didn't want him dead at Ryne's hand. Plus, if Ryne made a move, Dante would kill his mom. Ryne didn't need to carry that guilt into their relationship—if he still wanted one.

Ryne screamed in frustrated rage. He let loose both orbs of white light, exploding two trees on either side of Dante's head. To Dante's credit, he didn't flinch as the rest of the team had.

Ryne extinguished everything glowing about him and shook his head to regain his bearings. His chest heaved as he caught his breath. He looked at his mom, guilt obvious in his gaze, but at her encouraging nod, he rushed through the line of fire to Hollis, picked her up, and threw her over his shoulder. He carried her back across Roman's magical barrier and gently set her on the ground.

She leaned her forehead against his, both breathing heavily. "I'm so sorry, Ryne. We'll get your mom back, I promise." With her eyes she pleaded with him to believe her.

He gave her a curt nod in agreement. "We will."

Ryne gently grabbed her ankle and tried to examine her.

"I'm fine. It's just a scratch. I'll live, thanks to you."

"Let me fix it."

"Really, it's fine. I've had worse." She tried to bat his hand away.

Ryne's head snapped up, his eyes rimmed with red and filled with emotion, but his words remained gentle. "Let me . . . please."

Hollis acknowledged his need to do something—anything—and nodded.

"Are you going to cry tears on me?" Hollis cheekily asked.

Ryne laughed out loud. "No. I don't need to cry on you. I simply need to touch you with my blood or water from my body, and I can transfer some of that healing power to another."

"So like spit? You're going to spit on me? Well, what are you waiting for?" She winked at him. Finding humor in the moment seemed to help take her mind off the fact her own father had just tried to take her life and kidnapped her future boyfriend's mom.

He mischievously smiled, spat in one hand and rubbed it together with the other one, then placed his hand over her wound.

Concentrating, Ryne looked into her eyes. The outer edges of his were ringed with red once more, but this time he controlled it. When they both looked back at her ankle, the skin was healed and back to normal.

"Thank you," Hollis said. Her words were simple, but she pushed so much feeling and heart into them, he couldn't help but feel what she felt in that moment. "You saved me."

"I love you."

"Time to break it up. We're not done here yet," Macy warned as she and the others watched Dante and his group attempt to regroup and pull out weapons of their own. Nala pulled Ryne's mom back away from the potential action.

Hollis saw knives and a few other weapons, but when she saw one of the hunter's weapons, she started to panic again. "Gun! I see a gun!"

"You're up, Liberty. Move fast, Circe. I need you ready as soon as Liberty distracts them," Saundra directed. "Gallad, I want you to assist Circe's magic when she's ready. That line of fire won't hold for long."

"Not full force, dear. Just enough to bring them to their knees or distract them for what Circe will show their minds," Mathilde said, patting Liberty's hand before she stepped out. Liberty sashayed gracefully in front of the magical barrier still held intact by Roman. He and Lilith waited at the side. Roman ready with his magic, and she with a dagger in each hand. Without pause, Liberty opened her mouth and began to sing a beautiful song that grew in strength and sound as it traveled through the air. The benefit to being behind Roman's barrier was it protected the rest from the powers of her song. Dante and his team immediately covered their ears. Some fell to their knees, and by their reactions, Hollis would guess some were in various kinds of pain.

"Is she a siren?" Hollis whispered to Macy, who crouched by them.

"Not really. She's called a xana. She's a type of fae, but her song can affect evildoers like a siren's song would," she explained.

Just when the flames Ryne had set ablaze began to fade out, Hollis observed as Circe moved out of the protective barrier with Gallad at her back. Circe was petite with shoulder-length chestnut brown hair. Hollis took note how slight she was, but her size had nothing to do with the power she was about to unleash. She began to chant something under her breath, and the air around her shimmered in waves extending from her. Circe's magic was peaceful but powerful. Gallad came up beside her and placed a hand on one of her shoulders, lending her an extra push of his magic. The scenery changed as her magic pushed out farther and farther away from her. The sight was unreal as rocks and hillsides turned to plains and lakes surrounded by trees. The mountainous cliffs turned to hills in the distance. The scene looked like something from an entirely different location. Hollis could see Dante and the others become confused and disoriented. She heard their shouts of discord and frustration as they looked at compasses and GPS signals.

Hollis knew they had been spared—for now. It was only a matter of time before he tried again. Dante wouldn't let his vendetta drop. It would consume him until he died. He looked one last time in the general area Hollis and the others stood, watching. Then he rounded up his team and signaled them to head out.

Ryne started to follow after them, but Roman and Gallad held him back. The sight broke Hollis's heart. She stood and watched her father and his team go until they couldn't be seen as they disappeared into the small forest of the new landscape they saw.

Once they were gone, Circe dropped her spell, and the scenery changed back to the regular Colorado forest at the base of Mt. Sousa. Everyone breathed a sigh of relief. Roman, too, dropped his barrier, but Lilith refused to put away her weapons.

"Thank you, all of you," Hollis said with a rush of emotion-filled words. She couldn't believe it worked without them having to actually fight.

"Letitia's husband Tranner will follow them from the sky." She turned to Ryne, steely determination in her eyes. "We will not give up your mom without a fight, I promise you that." Saundra sighed.

"For now, it's time to go. I have vehicles waiting," she called out, and everyone followed her back to the road.

Ryne acknowledged her words with an appreciative nod, but couldn't take his eyes away from the last spot he saw his mom being yanked back into the forest with the rogue hunters.

"What is Tranner?" Hollis asked Macy with a confused whisper as she watched Ryne with concern.

"He's a dragon shifter," she explained.

"Of course he is." She let the others get ahead of her as she slowed down in thought. But before Hollis got too far, she saw a shock of blond, curly hair peek out from behind a large tree trunk. She hissed in a breath of surprise.

"Sunny!"

The bright blue-eyed girl about the age of thirteen or fourteen—no one knew for certain—came out from behind the tree with a big smile on her face. She innocently skipped over to Hollis like nothing had just happened.

Hollis's gaze shot all around them to make sure no one else was there. She reached out with her hunter senses, but they were the only ones left.

"Don't worry. They're gone," Sunny confirmed.

"You shouldn't be out here all alone," Hollis chastised. The girl just smiled at her.

"Macy said that to me once before, too. Someday you will all learn, I'm fine." She rolled her eyes as if having to explain things to adults was exasperating.

"What are you doing here?" Hollis asked.

The girl's eyes roved over to see Ryne standing next to Hollis, a flame of fire hovering in his hands, ready to protect her if needed. Sunny smiled even bigger than before. "I wanted to meet him!"

The flames in his hands died out, and he inclined his head. "I'm Ryne."

"I'm Sunny, but you knew that by now." She turned to Hollis and stared into her eyes. "You're happy now. So I'm happy. He'll take care of you."

With emotion in her eyes, Hollis couldn't help but smile up at Ryne. She knew Sunny's words were true. Turning back to the girl, Hollis had an idea that lit up her eyes. "Sunny, come back with us. You don't need to stay with Dante. You can live with me."

Sunny gave Hollis a big hug. "It's not my time yet."

She turned and left. A young, seemingly innocent girl in a yellow dress skipped unafraid through the dangerous forest all alone at night. Hollis shook her head and chuckled at the absurdity of the sight.

"Whoa! Is she for real?" Ryne asked with surprise.

Hollis nodded. "She's special. No one knows her true story. She's a hunter, but she's something else as well. I don't think she even knows. But for some reason, and I'm betting it's not good, Dante keeps her around and humors her childlike innocence. She was the only one I really ever felt connected to."

"Should we go after her?"

Hollis watched Sunny turn around and wave in the distance before she could no longer be seen.

"No. She'll be fine. We'll see her again someday. She runs on her own timetable." Hollis laughed at her own words. It was true but to anyone else she would sound crazy.

Ryne put his arm around Hollis's waist. Everyone else had gone. "Ryne, he won't kill her. She proved her value to him in finding Havenwood Falls. And now she's leverage. I promise you we will find her—and Dante will pay."

He kissed the top of her head. "Let's go home."

"Home." She sighed contentedly for the first time ever. "I like the sound of that."

Hollis snuggled into his side. Ryne tossed a fireball in his free hand like it was nothing. She laughed. "Look at you! Figured out how to merge your magic with your phoenix and just like that, you're an expert."

"It was because of you. I have never done what I did tonight before. I can't wait to tell Ember about it. She won't believe I did it."

Then growing a bit cocky, Ryne tossed a fireball a little too high and almost missed catching it.

Hollis laughed deep from her gut. "Don't burn down the forest or we'll be kicked out of town for sure!"

He extinguished the fire, and they walked hand in hand back to the car. Saundra, Roman, Lilith, and the others waited for them.

"We'll be shortly behind you," Saundra said as she closed the car door. "Be at Court chambers tomorrow morning."

Hollis and Ryne joined the others and were driven back to Havenwood Falls, back to their home.

"I wonder where the elders are going," Gallad said, staring out the car window after them with a pinched expression on his face.

"I don't know. I'm sure they'll tell us later. We're safe again for now," Macy said with relief.

"For now," Hollis echoed. Concern for what would happen next with her father and also with Ryne's mother weighed heavy on her chest. The night hadn't been a victory, but they were able to buy some time, at least.

EPILOGUE

"Have a seat, Hollis," a stodgy older man with pale green eyes and wild white hair directed the next morning in Court chambers. He hadn't been present the last time she had been in front of the Court, but his name plate said *Lawrence Mills*. She took the seat she had sat in before, and Ryne sat behind her. Hollis immediately found Macy and Gallad seated in the audience. Addie sat in what must be her usual seat in the back, ready to take notes. Letitia and Eva Blackstone were also present.

Roman Bishop and Lilith were mysteriously absent from their Court seats, but Mathilde, Michaela, and Saundra were familiar faces, as well as Elsmed—who she came to understand was fae—and another woman whom she didn't recognize with a name plate indicating her as Barbie Stuart. Ryne told her Barbie was the mayor of the town and the only human on the Court.

"Let's begin," Saundra said, unnecessarily striking her gavel. "I hold Lilith's vote. Elsmed, you have Roman's?" Elsmed slowly nodded. "Mathilde, you have Odette's, and Michaela, you have Siobhan's vote."

Mathilde turned to Hollis. "Hollis Blackstone, you came to Havenwood Falls under false pretenses. You have since then selflessly helped to protect the town from danger. As for Dante Blackstone, he has been dealt with, thanks to you. This is a small trial to test your true intentions as of this moment. Will you agree to this test?"

Hollis paused at Mathilde's comment regarding Dante but figured she could wait for another time to ask her about it. She looked them each in the eye. "I will."

"Do you plan to harm the people of this town?" Saundra began.

"No."

"Do you intend to divulge the location or secrets of this town and its people?" the grumpy man, Lawrence Mills asked with a gravelly voice.

"No."

"Will you continue to protect this town and our people?" Michaela took her turn.

"Yes. I will."

"Why are you choosing to stay here?" Mathilde then asked.

Hollis took a deep breath and looked over at Ryne then smiled. "I have found where I belong. My heart has chosen Havenwood Falls and Ryne Calloway."

Hollis turned back to the Court and winked at Michaela, who was smiling at her. Mathilde cleared her throat. "Elsmed, what say you?"

Elsmed nodded. "She passed."

Hollis figured he must have some kind of lie-detecting gifts, being fae.

The gavel struck the wood. "Time to vote. All in favor?" Saundra called and noted the hands raised. "All opposed?" Saundra looked to the Court.

Saundra struck the gavel once more. "Congratulations, you are now a member of Havenwood Falls, providing you agree to our final stipulations. The first being the spell we spoke of last night to ensure your life essence is disguised from Dante. And the second, you receive your registered tattoo completed by Addie at the close of this meeting. Do you agree to our terms?"

"Yes, I do," Hollis answered. She glanced out at the audience and noted Lilith sneaking into the audience late. Her usual uptight, put-together self was lacking, and there were dark circles under her eyes. Hollis wondered what she got up to the rest of the night.

Mathilde, Saundra, Addie, Gallad, and other witches Hollis had felt hiding in the shadows stood up. Even Ryne stood up behind her. He was after all, half witch. "The spell is simple but requires a great deal of magical energy. We have invited members of the Luna Coven to assist us. It will not only bind you to Havenwood Falls unless provided with a leave of absence by the Court, but will also sever your tie to your old life."

"What do I need to do?" Hollis asked. Her skin practically crawled with all the witch energy flooding the room. She felt herself on the edge of control, but miraculously held it together.

"Nothing. Just allow the spell to take root in your soul," Addie interjected with a reassuring smile.

"What you feel is your raw hunter side emerging because of the power. Once Addie completes your tattoo, it will provide an extra cushion of protection from the effects witch magic has on you," Mathilde explained. Hollis couldn't speak; she could barely nod, the feeling was so intense.

"Just do it," she chattered out between her teeth.

The witches chanted in unison. Their voices grew louder with each new phrase. The power was intoxicating and overwhelming. Hollis felt the spell circling her body, seeking entrance. She closed her eyes and opened her soul, coaxing her body to accept it. She thought of Ryne, and her heart swelled with love. The spell took root, and she gasped at the instant connection.

As soon as it started, it was over. She sighed with relief and took a moment to catch her breath.

"And now, Addie, please do your part," Saundra instructed. "This concludes today's session." She struck the gavel once more. On cue, the rest of the coven filtered out of the room, and the Court stood and gathered their things to leave.

"Go ahead and sit, Hollis. We can take this part a bit slower," Addie said as she sat next to her and got out her tools.

"We just do this right here?"

Addie smiled. "I can do it anywhere. Do you know what tattoo you'd like?"

"I get to pick?" she asked with a smile.

"You bet! So make it a good one," she said with a wink. "But if you don't know, I can come up with something. It's my specialty."

Hollis shook her head. "I know what I want."

"I figured you might."

The tattoo only took Addie about an hour, and when she was finished, Ryne was waiting for her.

"What did you get?" Ryne asked, rubbing his hands together in excitement.

She peeled back the gauze from her wrist and held it out for Ryne to see. It wasn't big, but it covered her entire wrist, over the place where her tracker was embedded. Ryne couldn't take his gaze away from where he gently held her wrist.

"Ryne? What do you think?" Hollis asked, trying to see into his eyes. When he didn't respond, she looked to Addie for help. Addie only shrugged as she packed up her tools.

"Ryne?" she asked again more softly.

He lifted his head, and with tears in his eyes, he said, "You got a phoenix with magical sparks. For me?"

Hollis nodded, suddenly unsure of her choice.

Ryne grabbed her face with both hands and brought her in for a kiss that took her breath away. When he pulled back, she laughed. "So does that mean you like it?"

"I love it. It's beautiful with its feathers and the flames shooting out from it. And the magic sparks actually shimmer." He looked to Addie. "You did an amazing job as usual, Addie."

"She knew exactly what she wanted, which always helps the artist, but thank you."

"What's this word? Is that Latin?" Ryne grabbed her wrist again and studied it.

"It is. It says: *redefined.* It means I get to decide who I want to be from now on," Hollis quietly said, touching the necklace at her neck that inspired her.

"Perfect," Ryne whispered and kissed her hand.

Addie walked with them as they all left the chamber.

Roman Bishop, Lilith Blackstone, and Saundra Beaumont stood outside, apparently waiting for them.

"I trust your registration is all taken care of?" Saundra asked, looking between Hollis and Addie. Hollis nodded and held up her wrist with the bandage back in place. Saundra nodded.

"Mrs. Beaumont? What did you mean when you said Dante had been dealt with in there today?" Hollis dared ask.

Lilith stepped forward at Saundra's gesture. "Hollis, with the help of Tranner last night, we tracked Dante back to where they were staying and apprehended him. We now have him in custody, in preparation to have him sent to the Infernum."

Hollis knew they all watched her for a reaction, but she didn't give one. Instead she deeply inhaled and briefly closed her eyes. Upon opening her eyes, she offered a sharp accepting nod.

"If you would like to say goodbye, we could arrange that for you," Saundra offered.

"That won't be necessary," Hollis replied. "I said all I needed to say last night."

Ryne cleared his throat while eyeing Roman suspiciously. "What about my mom?"

"Did you find her? That would be the only reason I'd talk to Dante," Hollis interjected.

Roman and Lilith glanced at each other for a suspenseful moment, then moved apart, revealing Ryne's mother. She appeared exhausted, drained, and disheveled, but she wore the brightest smile on her face with tears of happiness trickling down her cheeks.

"Mom!" Ryne rushed in, picking her up in a big bear hug and swinging her carefully around. "You're here! Are you all right?" He didn't let her go so she could answer, but Hollis smiled at her tiny nods compared to how big he looked holding her. Once he finally put her down on her feet, he looked to Roman, then to each of the women there. "Thank you for saving my mom. You don't know us well and yet you treated us like family, like we mattered, more than any of our actual family ever did. Thank you."

"In Havenwood Falls, you are family," Saundra said with a smile.

"Welcome home, Hollis," Lilith said. "We expect to see you at the house for dinner on Tuesdays with the family, and I'm pretty sure Letti is going to put you to work at NamaStays."

Hollis smiled. "I'll be there, thank you."

Lilith turned and departed to the waiting car across the street, where Reggie stuck his hand out and waved at Hollis.

Roman, too, turned to leave, but before he did, he stepped back to Hollis. "Remember this favor in the future, witch hunter. I will collect."

Hollis gave him a curt nod and he left. She knew he was only invested for something he might need in the future. But today she didn't care.

"Come on, Mom, I'll take you home," Ryne said, with his hand steadying his mother's elbow. "But first I want you to meet someone." He brought her toward Hollis with a big cheesy grin on his face.

"We can do this later, Ryne," Hollis offered. His mom looked like she could use a long nap, a feast, and several showers.

"Nonsense," his mother interjected. "I've been waiting a long time for this day. You were very brave last night to stand up to your daddy like that, young lady. My Ryne is a good judge of character. I'm Jessica Calloway."

"I'm Hollis." Hollis actually blushed. She had never met a guy's mother before.

"Well, that made my job easy." Ryne chuckled. His mom swatted him in the chest.

"Ryne, you stay with Hollis. Saundra has offered to take me home and inspect me to see if I need healing. Come by later, both of you, when I've rested."

Saundra took Nina's other arm and helped her into a car. Ryne watched as they drove off.

"She'll be fine, Ryne. I could see her already growing stronger the longer she's been in Havenwood Falls," Addie supplied. "I'm off too. See you both around."

"Bye, Addie, and thank you," Hollis said with a smile.

"Ryne, get her a new phone and then give her my number. I'll get Callie and Michaela, and we'll go out for drinks some night."

Hollis stopped in her tracks and smiled. "I'd like that."

"Wow, you already have friends," Ryne said, smiling at her.

"And a boyfriend too." She winked at him.

"Shit, you work fast, woman!"

"Today is a good day. Your mom is safe and home. Dante has been stopped. And I get to start my life fresh."

Before she could say anything to continue their banter, Ryne scooped her up in his arms and carried her to his truck.

"Put me down! Where are we going?" she said, laughing the whole way.

"Well, I figure if I've got a girlfriend, I'd better take her on a proper date." Ryne smiled and leaned in toward Hollis's face staring up at him from his passenger seat.

"I guess so," Hollis said as she pulled Ryne down toward her and threaded her fingers through his dark hair. Hollis kissed him slow and sensual, biting and nibbling his lip. Ryne groaned and deepened the kiss.

"But first take me home."

～

We hope you enjoyed this story in the Havenwood Falls series featuring a variety of supernatural creatures. The series is a collaborative effort by multiple authors.

Books by Morgan Wylie in the Havenwood Falls world:
Reawakened
Dawn of the Witch Hunters
Redefined
Rise of the Witch Hunters

Rediscovered

Also look for the YA line, Havenwood Falls High; the historical paranormal line, Legends of Havenwood Falls; the sexier side of town, Havenwood Falls Sin & Silk; the local supernatural college, Sun & Moon Academy; and the Havenwood Falls holiday short story anthologies.

Stay up to date at www.HavenwoodFalls.com

ABOUT THE AUTHOR

Morgan Wylie is an award-winning and *USA Today* Bestselling Author with several genres published from YA fantasy to adult paranormal romance, as well as other stories in between. Morgan published her first novel, *Silent Orchids,* one year after moving across the country with her family on a journey of new discovery. After an amazing three years in Nashville, Tennessee, and the release of two more books, Morgan and her family found their way back to the Northwest, where they now reside. With a collection of twelve-plus titles, she passionately pursues working every day with great optimism. Daily, Morgan continues to embrace all things: Mama, wife, teacher, and mediator to the many voices and muses constantly chattering inside her head, where it gets pretty loud!

You can find her and news on her books at the following:
MorganWylie.net
Morgan Wylie Books on Facebook
@MWylieBooks on Twitter and Instagram

ACKNOWLEDGMENTS

I have loved every minute I get to spend in Havenwood Falls! Not only has it been an amazing place to write and create for, but it's been such a fantastic experience to work with so many amazing and talented authors. Thank you to Kristie Cook for following your heart and creating such a magical place for us as mere humans, and for the characters we've grown with, to hang out. Thank you to all the authors involved with Havenwood Falls even if I didn't have the opportunity to collaborate with you on this story specifically. You are all an inspiration to me.

Specifically I want to thank Kristie Cook for letting me hang out with Michaela, Aurelia, Xandru, Addie, Tase and Saundra Beaumont. Thank you to Randi Cooley Wilson for letting me hang out with Callie, her consignment shop, and Roman Bishop. Thank you to E.J. Fechenda for the use of Willow Fairchild, her daughter Arabella, Harlow, Coffee Haven, and Elsmed. Thank you to Amy Hale for Lawrence Mills, Melissa Wright for Circe Alexander, Victoria Escobar for Liberty Veitch, Justine Winter for Shade StormIron, Nadirah Foxx for Montezuma "Monte" Tayute, Kallie Ross for Sheriff Ric Kasun, Tate Kasun, and the pack, Susan Burdorf for Rusty, R.K. Ryals for Harper, Amy Miles for Orlon Laroc, Ember Ramsey, and the rocs, and to anyone else I may be missing . . . Thank you!

Thank you to Liz Ferry for catching all the little things that slipped through, and helping my words flow smooth.

And thank you to the readers! You give our little town wings to fly and a voice to be heard. Thank you and keep reading!

AN EXCERPT

A Havenwood Falls New Adult Novella

HAVENWOOD FALLS

BETRAYAL AMONG THE FROST

AMY HALE

Betrayal Among the Frost (A Havenwood Falls Novella) by
Amy Hale

In this sequel to *Flames Among the Frost*, Jetta and Conrad are planning a wedding, but betrayals might destroy them before they can say "I do."

Jetta and Conrad's big day approaches, and like many brides, Jetta's feeling pre-wedding jitters, stemming from a lot of self-doubt. When her ex-boyfriend suddenly returns to town after a twenty-year absence, her concerns kick into high gear. His timing is suspicious, and her grumpy father, Old Man Mills, is unusually chipper. Something is amiss.

Jetta wants nothing to do with Turner Ireland, a fellow frost dragon. He left her years ago, and she's so over him. She just wants to focus on her wedding and begin her new life, but he refuses to leave her alone. Meanwhile, Conrad is willing and ready to do whatever is necessary to get Turner away from the woman he loves. But Turner's determined to claim what was once his.

A unique wedding, a persistent ex-boyfriend, an untrustworthy father, a jealous groom, and Jetta's penchant for disaster may just create the spectacle of the year—if the wedding happens at all. Betrayals and lies may just be the end of Jetta and Conrad.

BETRAYAL AMONG THE FROST

BY AMY HALE

Approximately one year ago

I walked into the disgustingly ornate room my father called an office and plopped myself into one of his overstuffed chairs. He didn't even glance up from his desk. Not that his blatant dismissal of my existence particularly surprised me. It's been this way since I hit my late teens. I once made the mistake of asking about my birth parents, and the old man blew a gasket. He couldn't believe I had the audacity to inquire about my origins. He'd since labeled me an ungrateful freeloader that needed to learn her place.

Fuck that noise.

I'd since made it my mission to annoy the piss out of him. And the news I'd just walked in with was likely to send him reeling. Since the chair I'd chosen was close to his desk, I stretched out my legs and rested my black boots on the edge.

"Jetta Mills, kindly get your repulsive shoes off my desk," he muttered without looking up from the paperwork he was writing on.

"Aren't you even a little curious why I'm here?" My feet stayed where they were.

He raised his pale green eyes to mine. "Do I want to know?" He looked at my boots. "I'm guessing I don't. Now move your feet, you insolent spawn." Lawrence Mills was never one to mince words. I took in his appearance. Today he wore a brown pinstriped suit that probably cost more than most people made in year. Wild white hair normally covered his head in more of an Albert Einstein fashion, but today he'd actually tried to tame it. It was combed back and almost looked mismatched with his crazy white eyebrows that still appeared to have a mind of their own. His skin was pale and creased with the wrinkles everyone expected from an eighty-something-year-old man. *He looks good for his age, considering he's really one hundred and ninety-seven.*

I chuckled. "Insolent spawn. I like that one. Your names for me are becoming more creative."

I sat up, placing my feet firmly on the hardwood floor.

He sighed.

"What do you want? I'm busy." The annoyed tone in his voice made me somewhat giddy. We were definitely heading for an argument.

"I'm getting married," I announced.

He dropped his pen. "You're what?"

"Married. You know, where you stand before a bunch of people and say vows, then fly off to Bora Bora to bump uglies."

He scrunched up his face in disgust. "Of all the . . . do you always have to be so crass?"

"Do you always have to be so cranky?" I tossed back.

"Whom do you think you're marrying?" He leaned his forearms on his desk and inspected me as if I were a nasty stain he couldn't vanquish.

"I *know* I'm marrying Conrad Monroe." I couldn't help the slight edge to my voice. It always pissed me off when he tried to run my life. I was a hundred and three years old, and he still thought he could tell me what to do.

"The lava dragon? You barely know him!" he bellowed as he got to his feet.

"We've been together for a few months now. I know enough," I stated calmly. I would not to let him get to me, and as a bonus, my lack of emotional response always made him angrier.

"Jetta Mills, I forbid you to marry that stranger." He started to pace the area behind his desk.

I rolled my eyes at him.

"I accepted his proposal shortly after we'd gotten rid of Brandt. I've been engaged for weeks now." I stood and put my hands on my hips. "It's happening. You don't have to like it, and I don't want or need your approval. I'm giving you notice as a courtesy."

"Damn it!" He grabbed his cane and pointed it in my direction. "Why can't you just be normal and obedient? You owe this family!"

"Because I'm not a dog. I don't live for your praise, nor do I want to be normal." I shuddered at that last word. Normal was so boring. "As for owing you, I'm sure I paid my penance years ago."

"Isn't there someone else you'd rather be with?" He stepped toward me.

"Like who? There aren't many dragons in town. And you know damn well you'd be having a fit if I were contemplating marriage to a vampire or fae."

"I've never forbid you to date either." He stuck his nose up in the air like a petulant child.

"No, you only forbade humans. But date is the key word there. You don't care so much when it's nothing serious, but the minute it looked like I might commit to someone, you worked to sabotage the relationship." I crossed my arms. "I'm not a fool. I knew what you were up to with past boyfriends."

He shrugged. "I was hoping you'd get all that wildness out of your system before you settled down with a good, respectable frost dragon."

I laughed. "All this wildness, as you call it, is who I am. Accept it or don't. But quit meddling in my business. I'm marrying Conrad, and you can't change my mind."

He took a deep breath and frowned.

"At least you're marrying a dragon," he grumbled.

"But you still hate him," I said with a matter-of-fact tone that didn't require an answer.

"I do. He's not Turner," he snapped.

"Not this again. Turner is the last person you should want me to be with." I felt my temper rising, and I took a deep breath to calm myself. I hated it when he brought up my ex. The guy was useless.

"Turner is a frost dragon and a proper mate for you!" Lawrence shouted.

"And the only boyfriend I've ever had that you liked. He's also an asshole and full of himself. If things had worked out between us, I'd be miserable." I looked at my father. "Not that you really care if I'm happy or not."

He harrumphed. "Marriage has nothing to do with happiness. It's about keeping the species going and our bloodlines pure."

"Well, shit. If that's all it is, I should have already been sleeping with every frost dragon I meet. I could just wander the town popping out babies and making more," I deadpanned.

"I didn't say you should be a whore." He growled, his pale green eyes almost glowing as he glared at me.

"You could have fooled me. Marrying for any other reason than love is whoring yourself." I moved to the doorway, fully prepared to leave. "I have too much self-respect to marry for less."

His cane wobbled as he leaned his weight into it. "If you had an ounce of self-respect, you'd be a different person than you are today. You don't look or act like a lady. You have the mouth of a sailor. And your choice of acquaintances leaves much to be desired."

"You don't like my friends?" I raised my eyebrows in mock surprise. "Well, pardon the fuck out of me."

"Watch your mouth, young lady!" he shouted.

I laughed. "Wait, you said I wasn't a lady. Make up your mind, old man. Am I a lady or a disgrace? You can't have it both ways."

He squinted his eyes at me and pointed a bony finger in my direction. "Mark my words, girl. You'll regret the decisions you've made. One day it'll all come back to haunt you."

"Uh huh," I said, as I brushed a piece of lint off my black T-shirt. "What are you gonna do? Cut me out of the will?"

He studied me a moment. "I just might."

"Well, there's a surprise. I honestly thought you'd already done that years ago." I smiled sweetly. "What'd you leave me, daddy dearest? A stick of gum?"

His bushy white brows drew together, and his pale lips puckered up in frustration. "I don't know why I bother talking to you. It's like trying to converse with a tombstone."

"I don't know. I only talk to you when I must. You seem to be the one that likes to keep it going."

He frowned as he hobbled past me and out the door, waving his hand in disgust as he left.

"Bah," he muttered, as he disappeared down the hall and around the corner.

~

Present Day

I sat at a small table in the back of Coffee Haven and looked at the pile of invitations stacked in front of me. A deep sigh escaped as I tried to clear my thoughts. How did I get myself into this mess? Many have never considered me the marrying kind of girl. I certainly wasn't the type you brought home to meet the parents. But there I was, stuffing wedding invitations into envelopes and contemplating the implications of just eloping. My fiancé Conrad wouldn't mind, but our friends and family would kill us. Not to mention it would be worth all the hassle to watch my frost dragon father bite his tongue as I said my vows. My father was a species snob and only approved of like marrying like. While Conrad was a dragon, he wasn't the right kind of dragon in my father's eyes.

Conrad's deep, masculine voice shook me from my thoughts. "You're smiling. What are you thinking about?"

"Hey there." I stood and kissed him. "I was just imagining the look on my father's face as we tie the knot."

He chuckled. "You do love pissing him off."

I sat back down and picked up another invitation.

"You know what they say—if you're passionate about something, do it. And I'm good at making that old man see red." I smiled wickedly.

Conrad chuckled. "You enjoy harassing him way more than you probably should."

I pointed an envelope in his direction. "You didn't grow up with the old turd, so no judgment out of you."

He held his hands up in surrender. "Nothing but love and respect here, babe."

I smiled up at him. "You're sexy when you're bending to my will, you know that?"

I took a sip of my coffee.

He smirked as he looked at his watch. "Is that so? I wonder if that works the other way around. I'll make a list of ways I'd like you to bend later."

I choked on my coffee at his double entendre. Every patron in the shop turned to look at me.

I took a moment to catch my breath. "You may be the death of me. You love to catch me off guard."

He leaned down in front of me, placing his palms flat on the table. His eyes were level with mine.

"That's part of the fun." His gaze traveled to my lips. "You missed a spot." He leaned forward and sucked my bottom lip into his mouth, removing any coffee that remained.

My will to become a respectable citizen in Havenwood Falls was quickly slipping away. I pulled back just enough to look into his eyes once more and whispered, "How much would it destroy our reputations if I tossed you on this table and proved to everyone that internet porn isn't nearly as interesting as we are?"

His smile was wide. "It would probably totally decimate any chance we had of a fresh start. Not that we really care, but . . ."

His eyes blazed with heat, as if he were challenging me to go through with it.

Temptation was staring me in the face.

Closing my eyes for just a second, I took a deep breath. I planted a quick kiss on his lips, then sat back. "It'll have to wait. I promised I'd meet Bianca here to discuss wedding plans."

The thought made the butterflies in my stomach return.

He made a pouty face. The kind that looks utterly ridiculous on a man. "I'm heartbroken. I never thought I'd see the day when flowers and invitations would be more important than me."

I shook my head. "I don't really care about that stuff, but Bianca does, so I'm doing this for her."

He stood and smiled. "I've got to meet Ms. Collins anyway. She's wanting a bid on repairing her kitchen cabinets. Don't let Bianca talk you into any pink shit."

I snorted. "Never."

He stepped behind my chair, then leaned down where his lips brushed my left ear. "I love you. Enjoy your time with your sister-in-law, and I'll enjoy you later."

He placed a hot kiss just behind my ear, and a shiver ran down my spine.

"I love you too," I whispered.

As he walked away, I focused my gaze back to the invitations. I had most of them stuffed and ready to mail. I loved him. I wasn't lying about that. I wanted to spend the rest of my life with him. But the closer the wedding came, the more uneasy I grew. I needed to figure this out before I did something that would ruin Conrad's life.

I was afraid of destroying his future. He deserved every happiness—a loving wife, a house full of kids, the whole nine yards. It worried me that I might not be able to offer him that. What did I know about family life? Someone had left me on Lawrence Mills's doorstep when I was too young to remember my real parents. Lawrence's wife Christine Mills passed away years before I was even born, which meant someone left my upbringing to a very cranky old frost dragon and a sweet but somewhat distant older brother. I had no role model to mold my idea of a wife or a mother. My sister-in-law Bianca was fantastic at both positions, but I'd only known her as a wife and mother for a short time, since she and my brother ran from Havenwood Falls shortly after they married. Another absence in my life I can attribute to my father. Thankfully that loss was only temporary, and they'd come back home several years later.

The idea of being a mother terrified me. I couldn't imagine myself in charge of assuring another being stayed alive, let alone thrived. And Conrad wanted kids. His life up to this point had been devoid of family connections, and he wanted to change that. Surrounding himself with people he loved and who loved him was a goal. I understood that, but I worried I wasn't the right one to give it to him. What if I screwed it all up?

Being a wife wasn't quite as scary, but I still worried I'd disappoint. What if I didn't meet his expectations? I often fell far below the standards of many. Expectations were a lot of pressure.

I looked up from the table to see Bianca heading my way. I pasted on a smile I didn't quite feel. "Hey there. Glad you made it."

She blew out a frustrated breath. "Yeah, sorry I'm late. Zoey had a minor teenage meltdown about her plans with Jordan for July fourth, and I had to keep her from losing it. The last thing I need is her shifting in the living room and then trying to explain to the neighbors why a large dragon was destroying my house."

I chuckled. "Yeah, that'd make for interesting gossip in the HOA meetings."

She shook her head. "I love that girl to the ends of the earth, but she knows how to try my patience."

I swallowed hard. Bianca had the patience of a saint. If she struggled with motherhood, how would a hothead like me ever make it work?

"Anyway, enough about that. Are you ready to pick out flowers?" The excitement in her voice helped me forget my worries momentarily. Bianca's eyes lit up when I originally asked for her help to plan the wedding. I had no idea what I was doing.

"I am. What are you thinking?" I took another sip of my now cold coffee.

"I was thinking—" She froze. "Oh my god."

"What?" I frowned at the expression of disbelief on her face. Her eyes looked past me, focusing on something in the background. I was about to turn and look when I heard a voice I hadn't heard in years.

"Hello, Jetta. It's been a long time."

Turner Ireland stood beside our table. He looked just as I remembered him all those years ago, with only a slight hint of maturity aging his features. And it appeared he'd spent some time in the sun, which was odd since frost dragons didn't tan. He had to be spray tanning. He smiled down at me, and all I could do was stare in response. He pulled a chair up, flipped it around backwards, and sat down. Blond hair sprinkled his lean, muscular arms that he crossed over the back of the chair as he leaned forward.

"Nice to see you again, Bianca." He glanced her way.

She nodded. "You too."

He smirked, a small chuckle escaping his lips. "You never could lie well."

Bianca looked at me and blinked rapidly. Her confused face echoed the thoughts racing through my mind. What the hell was Turner doing back in town?

He turned his gaze back to me, and I could almost feel his bright blue eyes roaming over me. "You look amazing, Jetta."

I opened my mouth, willing anything remotely intelligent to come out. "Oh. Thanks," was all I managed. I frowned. "What are you doing back in Havenwood Falls, Turner?"

He shrugged, the motion causing his blue button-up shirt to pop open at the neck, revealing more tan skin beneath. "I needed a change of scenery."

I raised one eyebrow. "When you left twenty years ago, you said you hated it here."

"I thought I did. But time changes a person's perspective. I've very recently realized that I've never really been happy anywhere but here."

I chewed on the inside of my cheek, a nervous habit I hadn't had in years. *Damn you, Turner.* "Well, welcome back. Bianca and I have some important things to discuss, so if you would excuse us, we need to get back to it."

He stood. "Absolutely. I just wanted to come over and say hello. It's good to see you again, Jetta." He glanced at the pile of envelopes on the table but made no comment other than "I'll see you around." He walked to the counter, picked up an order to go, and left.

Bianca sighed. "Wow. He's just as hot as he was when you two were together."

I stared at her. "Really? That's all you can say?"

"Sorry, I'm still in shock, I think."

I glanced back at the door, assuring myself that he had left. "I can't believe that just happened."

She reached out and put her hand over mine in a comforting gesture. "Are you okay?"

"Sure. Why wouldn't I be?" I tried to brush off her concern.

"Hello? Because Turner was the love of your life once. You were together for years."

I stacked the invitations into a neat pile. "I'm fine. I'm just surprised, that's all. He means nothing to me anymore."

Deep down I prayed that was true. When he left, it crushed me. Seeing him again drudged up a lot of uncomfortable emotions and issues I'd just as soon forget forever. And it appeared those issues were staying in town for a while.

Purchase *Betrayal Among the Frost* where books are sold.